Fateful Chance

WORKS BY SYK KELLY

CRUEL GODS SERIES:
BRINGER OF DEATH

CRUEL KINGDOMS SERIES:
SINISTER DESIRE
FATEFUL CHANCE

CRUEL KINGDOMS

SYK KELLY

DEDICATION

For all the little Reapers who've imagined that phantom waiting for you in the corner of a dark room, who had that voice in the back of your head telling you it isn't real. That voice lied.
He's very real.

CONTENT WARNING

This is a dark romance novella containing the following trigger warnings: somnophilia, breath-play, attempted sexual assault, physical assault, masks, stalking, kidnapping, CNC/dub-con, off-page torture, poison, and murder.

Chapter One

The low humming melody is always the same at these balls. It starts with a slow, deep, soul-summoning vibration that's ruined by the upbeat violinist, pianist, and array of other instruments merging into one belting ensemble. Everyone dances, jumps, twirls, and pretends to touch one another, just out of reach, only to come together at the end until the crescendo of applause fills the great hall.

It's all a bore. Some played out romantic fairy tale told in the form of a dancing lullaby.

As a child, I loved to watch the dances, loved to practice with my older brother, Cain, for the chance to one day dazzle someone with my perfect form and grace.

A child's dream.

As if love could be as simple as dancing. Maybe I should saunter around and inform the masses that romance is dead. A lie we gaslight ourselves into believing to make us feel better about dying alone.

It wasn't until after the *incident* that I became this grim, turning in my romance novels and heels for daggers and sparring pads. It took years, but once I was able to attend the balls again, at the requirement of my father, I became a wraith in the shadows, a thorn in a bush, a paper on a wall. I can never remember the exact term. The point is, this is not my scene. I wear muted tones that blend in with the servants and huddle close to the nearest faux tree with a drink in each hand, far away from the pastel dreamers on the dance floor.

We could never fit in here. They're normal.

I shush away the voices in my head. They're not real, I know that, but no doctor, medicine, or witch has been able to fix me. My father spent a fortune over the last ten years trying, with no such luck. The only solution anyone has given me is to counter whatever negative thought I have and change it to a positive one.

For some reason, reframing that thought to: *These people are brainless marionettes who I don't want to fit in with,* doesn't sound so positive either.

Because it's a lie.

Says the imaginary voice, I bite back.

I spot my guard, Maison, by the entry doors. The soft smile he offers while in his statuesque, waiting position by the great, ornate candelabras gives me the sense of safety I need to remain where I'm supposed to and not run back home like a coward.

I won't fail tonight. I *can't*. Not if I want to rid myself of these voices once and for all.

Wait...

A sudden shiver runs up my spine. This place is as unsettling as the king who lives here: King Byron Whitehart. A man of few words who lost two wives in the span of a year.

FATEFUL CHANCE

It's believed this manor is haunted. The Whiteharts had hired maids who were never seen again, and the few who did manage to *escape* were never the same. It's said they went mad here by the restless ghosts who whistle, knock, and scream all through the night, taunting and terrorizing the poor women until… well, no one really knows. Maybe they ran away, maybe they died, or maybe they're still here somewhere and have no sense that they're part of the dreaded myths that surround the Whiteharts.

Since the latest escapees a few years back, King Byron refuses to hire women, claiming we're all too emotionally charged and easily spooked for his liking.

This elaborate winter ball is for his daughter, Aspen, the only woman who hasn't died or run off mad yet. Maybe, like me, she is but hides it well.

"Eva." Mel slithers next to me, adjusting the straps on her tight black dress, giving me the look that asks if her golden hair is still perfect and doesn't show the fact that someone had their fists in it five minutes ago. She has always been the rebellious twin I aspired to be until it cost me my sanity.

I give her a soft smile and nod that she's in the clear as usual. I'm not sure why my brother thinks she's cursed when she couldn't have more luck on her side.

"You mind passing me one since we both know you're not going to empty either?" She rips a flute brimming with champagne from my hand to replace her empty one while making herself comfortable on the wall beside me.

I rest my head against the floral wallpaper, ready for our own verbal dance. "This princess not to your liking? Or is it the lack of princesses that has your twat in a twist?"

"The second one," Mel sighs. "I much prefer sneaking into the false balls than these real ones, though the woman I just had wasn't horrible."

I nod in agreement. Not the woman part, but the ball.

These balls are for the real royalty to mingle, make alliances, and bargain for arranged marriages, while the false balls that follow months later are merely a show for the public. Our royal doubles play out the choices and agreements we make on these nights. My own double looks nothing like me.

Mel sighs again. "Most of the princes snuck off, and I don't blame them. These women are too bland and basic."

"Let me guess, like me?"

"You are the farthest thing from basic, sister." Mel swirls her drink lazily, taking in the crowd.

I frown, noticing the melancholy written all over her face. A face that's nearly identical to mine.

It's true, both of us are the farthest thing from basic. To start, our attire sets us and our entire kingdom apart from the rest. We don't sport the beautiful pastel colors or enormous dresses with wired skirts. We favor the vibrant dark dyes that most stray from: the simple, sleek, and comfortable fabrics that are more expensive than the others but cost less because of the design and lack of unnecessary accessories. It's a choice our father forced on us long ago to ensure we stand out in a crowd while also having the option to blend into the background as needed.

Be that as it may, Mel and I share entirely different personalities with few commonalities, one of them being our banter toward each other to see who will either laugh or stalk off first. Admittedly, it usually ends with me stalking off and Mel cackling like a maniac to herself.

Along with our faces, that is where our commonality stops. While she might laugh like a maniac, I am one. She doesn't hear voices, imagine a white-faced phantom following her around, or wake up to mysterious notes she wrote herself with pressed flowers in her diary. That's one thing she would never have either. She has always called me a trusting idiot for allowing my thoughts and feelings to be so easily read.

I raise a brow at my twin. "I'll pay you to dance with one man tonight." I hate the games Mel plays with men, but if it means brightening those sad eyes, it's worth the poor man's humiliation when Mel inevitably causes a disastrous scene for fun.

Oh, right. That's why Cain thinks she's cursed.

"She's a wretched witch who revels in watching the chaos she causes unfold around her." His words, not mine.

The worst was when she tricked a man into believing she was a witch. The man wet his pants when she started chanting nonsense.

"You forget yourself, Eva. I might favor one sex over the other, but that doesn't mean I won't have my fun. However, taking your money is of no interest of mine tonight." Her sights narrow on someone in the distance with her glass paused before her lips. This woman must be interesting to keep Mel from finishing her glass. "I was merely checking to see you haven't slit your wrists back here in misery. Now that I see you're fine, I have someone I need to introduce myself to."

"Happy hunting," I wish her, watching as she stalks off to someone I can't see, and wait to ensure she doesn't turn back.

I don't drink, but tonight is the exception. A homage of sorts. Tossing the flute back, I nearly gag on the tart flavor that turns my stomach.

This is the night I've been waiting for.

Twelve balls. Twelve princes to schmooze and entice over the last year until we reached this one.

I pat the knife tucked in the braid atop my head and the other snug in my chest. I give Maison one last look to make sure he doesn't see me sneaking away.

This bubbly could very well be considered my last meal if everything doesn't go exactly as planned, but one thing is certain: there will be at least one new ghost in this manor before the night is over.

— Chapter Two —

"I'm going to cut your little heart out, Evangeline."

Those words have rung in the back of my mind every morning and night for the last ten years. They're louder than ever right now. A repeated crescendo that won't stall until this is over.

I'm quiet on the balls of my feet, stalking down the hallway. It's like my own form of dancing: light on the toes, delicately sliding my hands along my partner—the wall—with every step and turn I make.

The maps I've been studying are only so helpful and don't take into account the useless paintings and decorated shelving I have to step awkwardly around while still maintaining contact against the wall. If anyone were to see me, they would think I took one of Mel's drugs, the one that makes her giggly and rub against every surface like it's velvet.

There.

The wall raises ever so slightly, breaking away from the rest of the flush wallpaper. With a little push the secret door pops back out, revealing the servant tunnels that appear to be abandoned, telling by the spider webs and lack of lit sconces.

For the first time in years, my growing smile isn't forced or fake.

I made friends with the darkness long ago.

Shutting the door back in place behind me, I creep down the tight walkway, dragging my hands along both sides of the walls in case of any unexpected turns. I have the maps memorized, but I won't chance any mistakes.

Three rights and a left later, the door is in front of me.

The peephole lets out a small glow of light from the other side. I'm two steps away.

And… still two steps away.

I don't know what's wrong with me. I can't move. My throat dries, glueing my tongue to the roof of my mouth. My heart pounds against my trembling chest.

He is probably on the other side, wondering what that loud thumping is. He's probably seconds away from pulling the door open, seconds from catching me lurking in the walls with weapons hidden around various parts of my body. They would sentence me to death without letting me mutter a lie to defend myself.

Coward.

I shake my head.

*I am **not** a coward.* I rephrase my thoughts. *I am cold and calculated, just as my father taught me to be.*

FATEFUL CHANCE

There are enough warm and fuzzy, soft girls in the world. They live for romance. I live for revenge.

This is what I've been waiting for, what I trained myself for.

Leaning forward, I peer through the hole, letting out a relieved breath when I find exactly what I'm looking for. *He* is lying in bed alone, his jacket hanging over the bedframe, his shirt opened down the middle while he lies on his back as if too exhausted to fully remove it.

However my father got the information is astounding. The smallest detail of the prince lying on top of the covers is spot on. Unfortunately for the prince and this kingdom, they have a rat willing to let him die.

As silently as I can, I press my fingers to the edge of the secret door and push, waiting for a squeak or noise that never comes.

I abandoned my heels in the tunnel, making each step quiet and effortless. It almost feels too easy. With every step closer, I grow more suspicious and paranoid that I'm missing something.

I am cold and calculated, I remind myself again.

I am unfeeling and… My breath catches in my throat as his face comes into focus. He's older now, but there's no doubt it's him.

Prince Silas.

The face I will never forget. A face branded into my very soul after being stuck in that darkness for over a year. The man who gave me the nightmares that plague me, the scars embedded deeper than my skin. My captor. My tormentor.

And he's just… sleeping.

Forever if you get on with it.

He is so tall, I have to climb onto the bed and carefully straddle him to get the angle I need, keeping all my weight on my knees.

There are many blades hidden beneath my dress but it's the one inside the black braided crown atop my head that I reach for. The one with *S* etched into the hilt—another homage.

I'm carving your initials in my pommel so I can remember it was your heart I carved out, little Evangeline.

That dark and distorted voice rings through my mind as I tighten my sweaty grip on my weapon.

You are cold and unfeeling…

But he's warm and…

I pull my hand from where it fell to his chest and refocus, pressing the blade in the crook of his neck, right above his open collar.

His tan skin pinches, the vein throbbing against it, begging to be let open. I take a breath, then another. I can practically see a track along his skin, telling me where to slice him open.

"What are you waiting for, princess?"

I jerk back, heart leaping out of my chest. *No…*

The prince's striking hazel eyes meet mine. He catches my arm, quickly rolling his body over mine with my own steel now against my throat. "Were you planning on killing me, beautiful? Or was that your form of kinky foreplay? I'd prefer the latter for obvious reasons."

FATEFUL CHANCE

I struggle beneath him without saying a word. He's too heavy, and with my hands pinned above my head, I can't reach for any of my other daggers.

It's over.

I hesitated, and now I'm going to die. It would almost be better than facing my father, to see the disappointment behind his eyes at my inexcusable failure. I had one task.

The tip of my blade pinches beneath the black velvet choker around my neck, pulling the gold-set ruby forward. "I never thought I'd find Princess *Evangeline* in my bed. I'm not usually known for my luck."

I still.

The way he sings my name twists my stomach with knots of barbed wire. Of course he recognizes me. Now he can finish what he started ten years ago, cut out my heart as promised.

That very thing thunders like the storm on our way in, practically begging him to take it. "Just do it already." I bite through my clenched teeth, tightening my stomach to ready myself for the slicing pain that will end me.

Surprise flashes through his eyes, the glimmering hazel like lit kindling, ready to smother me with the intensity they possess. Something I wouldn't notice if I weren't looking directly into them.

The smirk on his face doesn't falter, growing more shrewd by the ticking seconds.

"Prince?" The door bursts open. "We received reports there could be an attack on your—" The guards stop. Taking in the scene before them, they both grip their swords. "Is this the assassin?"

This can't get any worse.

Think positive, Eva. This could very well get worse.

Silas narrows his heavy gaze back on me, keeping the blade tight against my throat. The man really does look exhausted, even his chocolate hair is tousled...

Focus, Eva.

That shrewd smirk grows wicked, slowly lifting up his defined cheeks. I don't like it one bit.

"Nonsense." He lets out a dark chuckle without taking his eyes off me. "This is my fiancé."

With the guards out of my view, I can't see their reactions, but I am confident I heard him wrong.

"Summon my father. This ball wasn't useless after all."

"Right away, prince." The door clicks shut. I move instantly, wiggling every part of my body to free myself of his unyielding restraint.

I realize too quickly it's useless. Silas is too strong and heavy. I haven't moved an inch and have only earned my wrists aching, promising bruises. I stop, huffing more frustrated with myself than the man holding me down.

"Do you speak, or does this thing keep you from it?" Again, he lifts the choker with the blade's tip, studying it with a curious glimmer.

"Why would you tell them I'm your fiancé? We both know why I came here." My throat tightens as the words tumble out. During my entire captivity I never got a chance to speak with him directly because of the bag that never left my head. If I dared to speak, plea, or so much as whimper, the punishments started, so I remained mute, living inside my mind with the voice that became louder—my best friend.

Awwww…

"Do you want to be my fiancé or my first death sentence?"

"I'd rather die than marry you," I spit.

He nods, considering. "I suppose that can be arranged. I'll let my father know when he gets here." He tucks the knife into his belt and removes his weight off me to stand. I don't get a chance to grab another weapon with the *try-it-and-you'll-regret-it* look he gives me. I know too well what this man is capable of to test his sincerity.

"While we wait, do you care to tell me why you planned to kill me?"

As if he doesn't know.

Key word, planned, because you failed.

I haven't failed yet.

Silas' brows pinch, studying me closer.

Bleeding thrones. I bite my lip to ensure my mouth isn't moving as the argument in my head unfolds.

Clearing my throat, I cross my arms and lean back against his headboard like I have no idea what he's talking about. "Do your guards often see you holding knives to women's necks?" I ask, curious as to why his guards would leave him with a person they believed was an assassin. They didn't even attempt to look around the room.

This kingdom really does not care for this man's—the *heir's*—safety.

"Do you often try to kill princes? I assume not since you're so horrible at it." I scold myself internally at the truth in his statement. He's not wrong; I hesitated. "You're really willing to die instead of marry me?" His head tilts to one side like I'm some puzzle he can't figure out. "Your brother married a common harlot. Your sister is likely not to marry a man anytime soon, not with the rumors about her. That leaves *you* left to marry a prince, *me,* who would bridge our two kingdoms together, making us both stronger."

I consider his words, almost forgetting who he is. Again, he isn't entirely wrong. My kingdom has always been outcasted, a target for wars that, thankfully, never started because we trade in secrets and make our moves in the background, undetected. But that can't last forever. A notion I told my father once before and earned myself two days in the tongue retainer to teach me to hold mine.

The prince drops onto the winged back chair and kicks his feet atop the desk without a care in the world—my life in his hands.

This would only be a failure if I died.

The door bursts open again.

Does anyone knock here?

I jump from the bed at the sight of King Byron Whitehart. It takes effort not to shrink into myself at the mere sight of him. He is older but one of the most handsome men I have ever laid eyes on, sharing an annoying resemblance to the prince, who is now standing at attention. The main, striking difference is the king has white slicked-back hair and a short, trimmed beard where Silas' is a dark mahogany. His stance is as pin-straight as his son's. His beady eyes are a shade lighter than the prince's darker hazel, and he looks at me with the same assessing amusement. "This is the one?"

"Yes, sir." Silas answers. "This is Evangeline Aramos."

"I know who she is, boy. The guards said you claimed she is your fiancé. Is this true?" The question is directed at me. Had I not grown up around royal men I would be more intimidated by this man. He holds himself with the physical power my father could never possess, but my brother does.

Straightening myself, I lift my chin high, like I always do in the presence of powerful men like him, ignoring the sinking feeling in the pit of my stomach. I give one curt nod. "Yes."

Failure isn't an option.

He holds my gaze, seemingly pleased. "You know his reputation?"

Everyone knows about the Damned Prince, where death and tragedy follow his every path. It's another reason I decided to rid the world of him once and for all.

I nod again.

"Precise. I like it. Normally women want to gab about how you met and how you got engaged. As long as you agree, I don't care." His grin isn't unkind, and yet there is a slyness I am familiar with. This man has something bigger at play with this information.

"Your father is going to be livid," he says, turning to face his guards. "Get her rooms ready across the hall and send word to her father right away. Her sister's here as well. Ready her rooms if she wishes to stay, too. Find their doubles and make sure they make a big show of the engagement."

Mel will be happy to sneak into the upcoming false ball.

"I don't need a special room for the night. We're leaving back home after the ball."

The king cocks his head as if I told an unfamiliar joke. "You're not leaving in the morning, Princess. This engagement won't be as long as usual, considering my son's constant defiance to find a wife. I won't take a chance on him changing his mind." His hands swing behind his back, making him taller and his chest broader. "This is your new home, Evangeline. The wedding will be in one month, and only because we have to get everything in order. If I thought this day would ever come, I would have actively planned for it."

His brow rises, and I swear there's a sympathetic look hidden beneath. "Fate has a cruel sense of humor, bringing you two together. The chances..." He shakes his thought away and clears his throat, correcting himself. "Why you agreed to this is something I can never understand, but I want to extend my sincerest gratitude. I've never been proud of him, but you gave me a semblance of that feeling today."

With that, the king leaves with the guards flanking behind him, leaving me alone with his son, who I attempted to murder less than ten minutes ago.

"Come to your senses after all?" Silas visibly eases back into the chair with his father gone. Horrid father at that.

It doesn't change anything. My father isn't a saint either and I didn't kidnap and torture a girl.

It could be the unfinished bantering with my twin or the fact that this man is so cocky and arrogant, it makes my blood boil, but I smile and mean every ounce of my promise, "I can't kill you if I'm dead."

Chapter Three

Behind closed eyes, I catch the moment the flickering candlelight dies out. The shadows take over, smothering me deeper into the warm mattress. It's not warm enough to keep the cool air from curling around me and prickling my skin.

I can feel him like I can smell rain coming.

The creek in the floorboards—my warning serenade—holds me in place and welcomes my skin with a warming blush.

I'm stuck between what's real and what isn't. The nightmares that plague me every night and the soft whispers pulling me out of them.

The brush of warm fingers against my cheek falls to the pulse along my neck.

I should have known leaving home wouldn't keep him away, or maybe it's them—the ghosts that reside within the shadows—craving what little life is left behind my flesh, clawing and seducing me to their side. A place I should have passed to long ago.

I'm in a haze between night terrors and dreams, mist and muscle, whispers and covered moans. I'm thrust back into the darkness with a deep, dark voice lulling me back to the other side.

"You shouldn't have come here, little Reaper."

"Marriage, Eva?! Like to be married with a husband and bearing little heirs?" Mel doesn't hide her distaste about the arrangement. Her whispers are harsh beside me, where we lie in the enormous feather-down bed. "Why would you agree to something so ridiculous? Is this a jest? Are you trying to out-jest me?"

I barely slept last night trying to find a way to explain this engagement to my sister, who doesn't have any idea about my task to kill the prince.

"He's handsome." I try to shrug casually but it's awkward at best.

Handsome is a tragic word to compare that man to.

Don't worry, he'll get tragedy, too.

Mel scoffs, unconvinced. "Evangeline, you are a heart-eyed, pining, secret romantic. You always have been. You would never marry someone for mere appearance. But…" She holds her hands up in faux defeat. "If that's the way you want to spin this, I won't pry. *For now.*"

I narrow my eyes on her. "Since when?" The real question is *why not,* but I catch my tongue before that slips and only further proves my displeasure with this entire mess. Nothing will change my mind from accepting this marriage, not when I still have to plan my next move to kill my *fiancé,* but if anyone had a chance to, it would have been Mel. Mel has a strange knack for convincing anyone into doing anything she wants. Something I'm surprised our father hasn't exploited, or if he has, I haven't noticed.

Mel rolls onto her back, taking in the intricate designs carved into the ivory ceiling. The room itself is a dream, fitted with an impressive four-poster bed, a wall-to-wall mahogany vanity with a matching formal table, and a wardrobe with far too many bright and saturated colors. It's the deep violets that paint the walls and duvet that throw me off. Princess chambers are typically filled with soft tones or pinks. I'm not complaining; violet is my favorite color, but I am surprised they have a room that suits me so well.

"Don't be mad, but I have to ask." Mel pauses. I already know what's coming. It's something I asked myself repeatedly last night, arguing with the voices on how to handle the situation. "What if you have a fit, or they get worse like fathers? You don't have someone like Mrs. Platewell who will take you away until you're better."

"I don't have fits like him," I remind her, as well as myself.

"You both hear voices," she presses.

"I hear my own voice, and I've never..." I tuck my head closer to hers, lowering to a faint whisper. "I've never hurt anyone, Mel."

"What about your Phantom, the white-faced man you see? If you start seeing him again..." The worry on her face grows more distressed. "It's snowing here, Eva. If you try to chase after him, you'll get sick or worse."

"I won't chase after him again!" My temper flares. It's rare I lose control but Mel is starting to piss me off. She acts like the voices and hallucinations are a problem. So long as I have a diary to dump all unwanted thoughts and feelings into, I'm fine.

The one time they've ever caused me trouble was when I was convinced my Phantom was real. I tried to chase after him, only to find myself panicked and delirious a mile away from home. I should have known he was a figment of my imagination when no one else saw him. Any time I turned to ask if someone saw him too, without fail, he disappeared. "I know he isn't real. If I see him, I'll chalk it up as an apparition. One of the spirits that haunts this place."

A smile threatens her lips. "I'm serious, Eva."

The smell of citrus and savory bacon fills the room, making my mouth water and my stomach grumble. In unison, our heads lift from our pillows, finding a full breakfast spread splayed out on the table next to the balcony's double doors.

"How long has that been there?" Mel asks, looking just as unnerved as I feel.

Not one to pass up an opportunity to eat, I toss the duvet and run to the table. "Quit your worrying, perk your tits, and let's enjoy this outside. I heard the winter sunrise here is to die for."

Literally.

I try everything while I'm layering a plate with French toast, bacon, eggs, toast, spiced jam, and sliced oranges.

"I can't say you didn't pick a good husband if food shows up without commands."

I don't disagree. Food is one thing I can never get enough of.

Grunting cuts through the chilly air, coming from down below where we settle ourselves around the balcony table. The sun grazes the horizon, casting early ambers, blushes, and hazy blues through the morning fog and dreary trees, reflecting too brightly on the new layer of fresh snow.

Our father trained us to be able to withstand the coldest temperatures, tossing us outside until our lips turned blue. He refused to have weaklings for children: no softness, warmth, intolerance to pain, or lack of knowing our surroundings, specifically people.

I let the chilly breeze, the smell of winter, and morning air fill me up before taking a bite of bacon and French toast, letting the sweet and savory mix perfectly in my mouth.

Peace. For a mere second, I feel peace with food in my belly and the sun on my face.

Until I see *him*, in the midst of the second thing I can't get enough of: fighting.

Silas marches forward in the courtyard below, shirtless with a sword in hand. The sweat glistens off every sun-kissed muscle, steaming and flushed red from the cold. With delicate precision, he wields the sword back and strikes down on the bulky opponent before him.

More grunts and groans ring with the strike of metal on metal. They both take a step back to rework their weapons quickly and bring them to blows again. Again and again, they step, slide, dip, weave, and slash. The opponent is much taller and stockier, which makes him slower.

Silas ducks and strikes the sword against his opponent's knee. When the man falls, Silas swipes the sword to his neck.

"You cheat!" The man scowls below him.

"You're big and slow, old man," Silas jests, offering his hand to the man, who doesn't look hurt at all.

Fake swords, then. *Pity*.

"You're older than me, moron." The loser pushes Silas' shoulder playfully. From this distance, it might only look that way telling from the way Silas stumbles back from the impact.

"That's Prince Holden, Silas' brother. Your soon-to-be brother-in-law," Mel explains, not having touched her food yet, while I look like a woman bewitched with the second piece of bacon hovering at my mouth. "They call him 'The Huntsman.'"

"Why?" I ask, not able to pull myself away from the scene: Silas smirking triumphantly at Holden, who stalks off harshly, clearly frustrated at being bested. *Sore loser*.

I tuck their interaction in the back of my mind.

"He hunts. Duh." Mel looks at me like I'm an idiot. Honest question, though, when my own nickname is the Vulture. Contrary to popular belief, I don't actually eat men. It's a metaphor for how I *eat them alive* in dagger competitions. "I can't see their faces clearly, but based on what I do see, I understand why you accepted Silas' proposal. Not my type, but I also wouldn't turn him away in bed."

I'm about to scold my sister for giving me that revolting image when Silas' chin lifts, his eyes clashing with mine. Before his smirk fully settles, I push my chair back and duck behind the railing.

"What are you doing?" The voice is much too light to be Mel's.

The woman standing in the doorway is about our age: pale skin, short black hair, and blood-red lips. She is no servant telling from her casual stance and open judgmental glower, though her cheeks are scraped with dirt and her dress is more common than royal.

"I…" I stand, brushing off my knees. I'm still in only a silk slip that reveals far too much skin. "I was looking for an earring I dropped." I sniff, whimper, and wipe away my commanded tears. "They were my mothers and I… I lost them."

Mel bites her lip to keep from smiling at the outright lie. It's our game, trying to get the other to laugh at the lies we make up for no reason other than to get the other to break.

The girl looks between us, spinning a silver band on her right ring finger. "Why are all the mirrors covered in your room?"

"Who are you?" Mel asks before I can, not bothering to hide her instant distaste for the girl. She's not one to share her feelings, but also not one to hide them so easily.

"Princess Aspen, the one whose ball you hijacked to snake your way into my family." I hold my face expertly still so as not to scrunch my nose at her accusatory tone. "I'm assuming the one that isn't a bitch is my soon-to-be sister-in-law? Silas doesn't typically favor aggressive women, though he also doesn't favor criers either, which begs the question, which one of you is Evangeline?"

Keeping my hands behind my back, a clear dismissal of introduction that should end this uncomfortable interaction quickly, I answer, "You can call me Eva."

"One of my seven guards is now yours, and a maid will help you with whatever you need."

"I thought you didn't have maids?" Mel, again, steals the question right out of my mouth.

"People also say we have ghosts and that our family is full of necromancers and witches. Just as it's said that your family is filled with vampires and werewolves, and while you both look like you could be brutal bloodsuckers, I doubt you turn into a wolf in the middle of the night."

I'm glad one of us is confident about that.

Both my sister and I tense, becoming hyperaware of the male presence that fills in behind Aspen. Our arms wrap in front of our chests that are barely covered by the thin slips. I swear the one with the big eyes keeps glancing at my breasts like they are made of the richest diamonds. My cleavage is generous but that doesn't mean I want this man showing his appreciation so brazenly.

"The guard will be posted outside your door. He's a bit grumpy, but he'll stop anyone from bothering you without your permission, unless it's myself, my father, or my brothers, of course. Your maid will show herself when she's needed. They're wonderful at staying out of sight and knowing when to appear as they need to." She carries on as if she is giving instructions to bake a pie and not flipping my entire world upside down. "You can do what you please today, as everyone is busy preparing for dinner, where we'll announce the engagement, but you are to stay within the manor until then. Do you have any questions?"

I offer her my best smile. If I'm going to infiltrate this family, I can't be prickly.

Before I can tell her that I have my own guard, Maison's mountain-sized presence comes up behind them and tells her for me, which she ignores with a roll of her eyes as she turns to Mel. "The bitch is Mel then. Your carriage is outside and ready to take you home. Your guard is already waiting outside."

Part of me wants to argue, to demand Mel stay here, but at least I have Maison. He's the only other person I've grown to trust. While I don't look at mirrors, he's mine, always telling me what I need to hear and not what I want, teaching me to handle a dagger and how to protect myself while taunting me about reading romance books when I don't believe in the notion of true love. I don't remember a day he wasn't at my side over the last ten years.

"I suggest keeping away from the basements. Holden is in a mood today and will be in there sharpening his tools or whatever for a hunt this month." Her lip curls toward Mel, giving her one last glance before turning harshly on her heel. The male presence leaves with her, and I don't doubt the promise of her guard outside my door. I would want eyes on a stranger in my home, too.

"I don't like her," Mel says once the door clicks closed. Aspen's soft humming fades farther away.

"An absolute cunt," Maison agrees, his mouth full while he nibbles through the breakfast spread.

"She's just particular and precise. Her father is the same way." It isn't uncommon for princesses to be standoffish, but most of us put on our fake smiles and say the pretty words we're all taught, '*nice to meet you*,' '*pleasure*,' '*thank you*,' and '*yes sir*.'

"She actually seems like someone from our court." Mel shifts her qualms to being mildly impressed. "Blunt and to the point with a hint of suspicion."

I laugh at the common descriptions of our kingdom. We aren't known for being pleasant and I'm in the home of the only other kingdom with a reputation just as horrid as ours.

Mel narrows her glare on the door. "That's exactly why I don't trust her. A fake smile and overused words are easy to read through, but someone rash and openly hostile will show you the knife while they have an assassin behind you with a sword already at your throat." Mel takes my hand into hers, her features tight and serious. "I mean it. Be careful around her."

"If you marry Prince Holden, you could stay here and watch my back for me."

Maison turns to us, bacon hanging from his lips with hurt behind his bright, cyan eyes. "What about me? I'm useless then?"

Mel scoffs with a twisted smile, her sharp teeth stabbing her bottom lip. Maybe Aspen has a point about us looking like bloodsuckers. "That brute of a man is the last thing I need, but if you want me to——"

"No!" I yell. "I was only kidding. You know I want you to find someone you like. Dare I say love?"

We both laugh. We gave up on that dream when our father punished us for having crushes that didn't benefit the kingdom, and again after our brother married for love. We both adore our sister-in-law, Audrey, but that punishment was particularly brutal, with scars on our feet to remember it by.

"You will not follow in your brother's footsteps." His bellowing voice is still sharp in my ear.

"Two down, one to go," Mel says, taking a bite of her eggs before turning into the washroom.

She's wrong. I don't plan to actually marry the prince, and I know Mel won't ever marry if she has a say in it.

With her gone, I tell Maison to stand guard outside the door, leaving me alone to rummage through the rest of the room. Everything is clean and bare except for the books on top of the vanity, next to the mirror I covered with the extra sheets. All of them look new and, at first glance, appear to be romance books. A quick skim tells me they aren't for children, however, one of them is different. The spine doesn't have a title but looks newer than the others, with no dust or worn cracks on the edge. I pull it out, finding the dark blue leatherbound cover also blank. When I flip to the first page, my heart stops.

A carnation is pressed against the paper with familiar scribbles.

The world spins around me, tunneling my vision.

I didn't know this was here… I don't even know where to find ink. I immediately spot the ink and quill further down the vanity counter.

I couldn't have… My mind wanders to the possibility I've persistently worked to rid myself of. But I don't think I can continue convincing myself that I'm the one who writes these notes. Not anymore.

I'm not sure Mel isn't right to worry about me when I see an entry in the new diary—one I swear I have never seen before—meant just for me.

Looks like you found your prince after all.
Tell me, will you still think of me when you're with him? Will you tell him
all of the dark fantasies you have hidden in that diary of yours? The ones you
*beg **me** for? Will you let him hold you between this world and the next?*
I still have the taste of you on my tongue, little Reaper. A new home won't
keep me away.

Chapter Four

Sending Mel off was bittersweet and harder than I thought it would be. Not because I'll miss her, that's a given. It's her warning plea replaying in my mind right next to the diary entry.

Little Reaper—that's what my Phantom calls me.

The doctors say the Phantom is me. They say I sleepwalk in the middle of the night and subconsciously write notes to make myself feel safe, that I imagine the white-faced man watching over me in the distance in public places like my own guardian angel. But if that's the case, why did I imagine him writing in my journal? Delusions aren't real and apparitions can't physically touch those who are alive, so how is it possible that I've imagined him touching me? I may have been too depleted after my training sessions with Maison, but I remember the feeling of his tongue between my legs. A feeling I can't consciously recreate to save my life.

I'm not sure what to believe. The fact that no one else has seen him makes it hard to trust myself.

You shouldn't. You're mental, just like your father.

FATEFUL CHANCE

He's not mental, he's...

Insane?

No! He's bitter, aggressive, impulsive, controlling... I'm just a little off. I'm nothing like him.

No matter how hard our father tried to make it otherwise, Mel has always been my rock, a laugh when I couldn't smile, a voice when I refused to speak for a year. Even now, she's a light without being here.

As I descend the obsidian stairs spiraling toward the basement, I imagine my twin beside me, keeping me from the voices in my head. I pretend Maison is at the top, waiting for us to return, and remind myself that the echo is supposed to be there, that those are my footsteps softly following behind me.

The sound of stone cracking ricochets through the frost-bitten air, alongside muffled grunts.

The lower I go, the colder it gets, my breath visible in front of me. The chill slithering up my back leaves goosebumps down my arms.

I recall one of the guests at the ball mentioning how a back-slithering chill is a sign of passing through a ghost. Another shudder runs through me at the thought of the dead and I sharing a body for the brief second it takes for us to pass one another.

If I were a ghost, I certainly wouldn't be wallowing in this wintry, direful manor.

That's not true; this is exactly where I would be, haunting the bastard who ruined my life until he's as deranged in the head as I am.

After I found the secret door to the servant's tunnels next to my bed, it was easy enough to recall the map I memorized and count myself to the basement stairs. The problem was passing Silas' room. My hand twitched to attempt another assassination, but I thought better of it. The opportunity will present itself again, I'm sure of it, and part of me needs to understand why he proposed this marriage after knowing I tried to take his life.

He's as suicidal as you.

I am not suicidal!

That's not what the doctors say.

Whoever found and returned me after my year in captivity decided to further torment me by leaving instructions to watch me closely for any suicidal tendencies. It didn't help that I clawed at my skin, still feeling the soft, tortured caresses of that damn feather.

I reach the bottom steps, in full view of the dimly lit room. The few candles cast more shadows than they do light. The gloom in this manor is truly unearthly and mesmerizing in a way that's not entirely unpleasant.

Holden stands in the center with his back to me, a sight that is much more impressive up close. From the balcony, I couldn't see how his back muscles flex with the slightest shift of his arms.

As he lifts a new dagger, I'm drawn away from his massive physique to admire the weapon he holds between two fingers. Swiftly, he tosses it at the wall, so hard it crumbles the stone it strikes before tumbling to the floor.

Rather than interrupt, I sit on the bottom step, observing him in his natural element when he thinks no one is watching.

Stalker.

FATEFUL CHANCE

He grabs two more daggers and strikes true in the circle drawn on the wall across from him. Sweat beads down his neck and back, giving away the hours he's been at this. That's the only explanation for the steam rising off his skin while I'm struggling to keep my teeth from chattering. I pull my arms around myself in a lame attempt to keep warm, but it's like warming ice with more ice.

"Do you want a lesson, or do you want to gawk like you did when we were practicing in the courtyard this morning?"

I don't say anything, unsure if he's talking to me or someone else. He has to be, right? With his back to me, how could he possibly know I'm here?

At my question, he turns his head with his right eye on me, and I think I might have asked it out loud. I've been known to do that. I bite my lip as if I can take it back.

"Princess?"

"It's just Eva."

"You're engaged to my brother, who goes by Prince. It's only fair you match the title in name."

Perfect, call me Princess, child abductor, torturer, monster, Evangeline, then.

"Like I said, it's just Eva."

His grin shows his perfect teeth. "Okay. *Just* Eva. Is it gawking or a lesson?"

"Gawking's been doing me just fine." I lean back on my elbows, resting them on the stairs behind me.

As much as I wanted to trust my father to gather intel, he doesn't have the same motivations I do for taking out Silas. I hired my brother's friend, Dove, to tell me as much as she could about this family before I came to help me plan how best to approach them if our paths crossed. She didn't know my plan to murder Silas, but she came through perfectly.

King Byron Whitehart needs silence and obedience, which he doesn't get from his children, specifically Silas. Aspen is the only girl and is treated like the princess she is with a very particular and precise attitude that rivals their father. Neither Dove nor I really know how to approach her. Holden is a hunter and little brother of the heir to the Whitehart throne. He wouldn't favor the pretty princess, polite type.

His deep laugh makes the room feel smaller than it is, solidifying my assumptions. He would trust someone who is more like him than not, and on paper, I am exactly like him: younger sibling to the heir of our throne, a wicked father, phenomenal with a dagger. I may not hunt animals, but I'm kind of hunting his brother.

Why didn't* he *ask us to marry him?

We're not here to marry!

"It's true what they say about your Kingdom. *Blunt and bold.*"

My stomach twists. "Please don't finish."

"But that's my favorite part. *Where whispers gather and hold your soul in tatters.*"

I jump to my feet. "Lesson it is. If only so I can throw it at your head if you repeat that again."

His grin doesn't disappear at the obvious threat. "I didn't realize you'd be so sensitive."

I grab a slim dagger from the table, admiring the neat, organized rows and slick metal gleam dimmed by the buttery flames. "I didn't know you'd be an asshole."

"I'd take your kingdom's rumors over mine."

"Fair and True?" I flip the steel in my hand, catching it by the hilt every time. Holden notes the movement, the precision I have without looking.

"With hearts so big, you won't see the knife behind you."

I choke on my laugh. "That's kind. I heard it was 'With hearts so big, their head can't be too.'" I bite my lower lip, making a show of raking my eyes up his solid frame, stopping at his chest. "I'd say my version rings true." I mirror his grin.

Shaking his head, he rubs at his wounded heart. "Silas is not going to know what to do with you."

"That's obvious." I turn and throw the dagger outside of the circle where a small crease has webbed its way up the wall. The blade sticks firmly in place. "The same can be said for you." I tsk. "Lessons certainly aren't it."

A slight blemish in the wall catches my attention. There's a secret door down here. We're already in the deepest level of the manor, I haven't a clue what could possibly be any lower.

There are rumors the Whitehearts found their wealth mining and built their castle over the old mining tunnels, but that seems too dangerous to be true.

It's just another piece of information I tuck in the back of my mind.

Holden takes a position against the wall, his arms crossed over his chest, watching me with a look bordering on impressed.

"Why don't you like your brother?" I ask. If he knows I'm bold, I might as well live up to the reputation.

"Who said I didn't?"

"It was obvious when you stormed off after you lost your sparring match."

"Because he cheats." That wry grin falls in place of a tight lip grimace. We're more alike than I thought, both ill-tempered by our siblings. "He knows we don't cut low during training."

"Why not? Shouldn't you practice every move, every angle, for any possible situation?" Why wouldn't they want to train to their full potential?

"You're just a girl. You wouldn't understand."

"Or maybe I have a full head with an actual clue." I bite back. "If you don't practice being hit low, then you'll get hit low and lose. You can't be afraid of getting hurt during practice when an actual war or attack could cost you your life."

His russet eyes narrow on me, his broad chest rising and falling with a deep inhale. "Do you fight?"

I plant my hand over my heart. "I am but a weak woman. I am surprised you would consider asking such an outrageous question."

"Fair." He nods. "I apologize for misjudging you and downgrading you by your gender. Our kingdom doesn't allow women to fight. I forget yours is strange."

"*Mmmhmm.*"

He pushes off the wall, heat radiating off him, melting the ice on my skin with every step closer. "It's hard to remember when you're dressed like that."

I glance down at my simple charcoal dress. "Like what?"

He looks me over in the same way I took him in a moment ago, making a show of trailing his unhurried observations from my ankles to my collarbone. "Like a woman trying to impress a man with her assets. I would say like the rest of them, but you are definitely *not* like the rest of them." His arm brushes mine as he reaches for one of the weapons beside me. "Color me impressed anyway."

My breath catches, sending a visible shadow of breath between us.

"My brother and I only have three things in common besides blood." His arms come to either side of me, caging me between them. He's so close, my back arches into the table.

"Food." *Same.* "Fighting." *Again, same.* "And Fucking."

My throat makes a loud, betraying sound as I swallow the saliva that pools beneath my tongue.

"You might act like a lioness, but you're just a little doe, aren't you, Eva?" He pushes off the table, the steel shifting behind me.

His footsteps echo up the stairs, leaving me alone to contemplate who won that interaction while struggling for air in the suddenly sweltering room.

Phantom

They say if you call on something enough times, visualize what you want, and speak it out loud, fate will find a way to gift it to you.

I didn't say a damn word, and yet my little Reaper was summoned to this place anyway.

The woman who nearly killed us both—my obsession—is here.

Not a single day has passed that the darkest parts of my mind haven't longed for this moment to come, though not under these specific circumstances. It's unfortunate enough that she found herself staying in this manor, but to be tied to the Damned Prince, damning herself to the reputation forever enmeshed to that name, is a waiting tragedy. A tragedy I'll ensure never happens.

She was never supposed to come here. She was to stay far away—safe—from this manor, from *me*.

She's a princess. She was supposed to find a prince, marry him, and live that happily ever after she used to dream about before the kidnapping. That girl was soft and naïve but overfilled with a lust for love and romance—of hope. After the kidnapping, she was a ghost of herself, a shadow of someone who no longer existed.

FATEFUL CHANCE

After she was rescued and returned, all I wanted was to ensure she remained safe and protected. Watching her from a distance was supposed to be enough, but I wasn't going to sit by and watch her become a living corpse, slowly dying after she survived that horrific year. No one was helping her, her father favored the other twin, her brother was never around, and her servants and guards didn't know what to do with her.

She didn't see me at first. I had my own eyes in that castle that reported back to me, and when they couldn't anymore, I used the hidden passageways to track and watch her.

I knew I couldn't directly tangle myself into her life, so I used her old diaries to communicate with her, leaving her notes to tell her she was safe, that she was okay even when I wasn't sure she was.

It took months for her to realize I wasn't going to kill her, only for those incompetent doctors to tell her that I was all in her head, that the pressed flowers and notes I left in her diary were her subconscious working to make herself feel safe, cared for, and seen.

I saw her. Not the normal girl she pretends to be for everyone, but the broken one she keeps hidden between the pages. The girl who hears voices and still wants to believe in love and happiness, no matter how much she tries to reject the notion.

She never writes about what she experienced while she was kidnapped, except for little hints: remembering feathers, darkness from the sack over her head, the ropes cutting into her wrists. Whatever that man did to her, he stole a part of her I've been coaxing back out for years—that damn hope.

The way her eyes light up and the crook of her mouth lifts to the sky after reading my notes or when she looks around after achieving a new skill with the daggers, it's all I need to know how starved she is for someone to truly see and accept her.

That little girl who dreams naively is in there, she's just been buried *deep* within the shell she's become.

With one hand behind my head, I settle her old diary on my lap and read the entry I've been flipping to find. The grin on my face spreads, remembering the first time I ever lost control and touched her. It's funny that she used to see me watching her from afar and think I was the one who kidnapped and tortured her, coming back to finish her off once and for all.

I did finish her off, just not in the way she expected. I couldn't help it.

At first, it was to soothe away her nightmares. She had been crying, tossing and turning, and scratching at her skin. I couldn't take it. I couldn't watch her harm herself anymore. I abandoned my hiding spot and held her until she calmed down.

Night after night, that became our routine: her flailing until I cocooned her against me. At one point, I thought she was doing it on purpose to lure me out, but after I read her diaries, I realized she had deeper fantasies than just being cuddled by her mysterious Phantom.

...the way he holds me doesn't feel fake. I feel his muscles beneath my arms, his breath on my forehead. I ache for more. It's wrong, even if he were real. No one should want to be craved so badly that they want to be taken without being aware. But when I start to wake up and feel his skin on mine, I heat in places I shouldn't, thinking that's exactly what he did...

The next few days, I watched her from dawn to dusk without much sleep. I watched her eat every meal. I watched her train with those daggers. I've always been drawn to her, have always wanted her, but something snapped after reading that raw side of her.

FATEFUL CHANCE

Watching her became less protective and more obsessive. The insidious proficiency she wielded a weapon... I had always studied her form and accuracy for ways I could correct, but she became more mesmerizing, in every sense of the word. Every time she held a blade, I couldn't look away. My throat dried, and my vision turned red, then black. My skin grew hot.

I lasted three days.

She had been lying in bed after a brutal training session, reading the *romance* book I left her. Her eyes had grown heavy, but her hand found its way between her legs. The way she writes it:

That book he left, or I guess, the book I found and forgot I put by my bed, affected me in a way no other book has. When I read the girl touched herself, I had to try it for myself. I've never done that before, but I wanted to see what sparks she felt. Is it real or something books make up? I was horrible at it. Everything was too wet and awkward. Until the white-faced man walked in. It took me imagining him touching me, his head between my legs, with his tongue doing what my fingers couldn't for me to understand what sparks the book was talking about. Only I wouldn't describe it as sparks, it was otherworldly, like I was suspended between veils, and my body couldn't decide if I should give up and pass already because there isn't a way I'll ever feel that again. No real man would want me if they truly knew me.

Grabbing the white healing mask, I place it on and take the secret passageways to her chambers.

Eva thinks she's too damaged with a reputation too tainted for any normalcy, that the voices in her head and hallucinations are too deranged for any man to want her, but she couldn't be more wrong.

If she wanted to keep believing the lies that love doesn't exist, she shouldn't have shown up here. My type of love isn't like the ones she reads about.

Seeing she's not in her room, I hurry to her bed and lift the mattress. The new diary I left her is exactly where I thought it would be, typical. Opening it, I press the viola between two sheets. It's her scribbles on the previous page that have me smirking beneath the mask.

~~Who are you?! Are you real? How are you here?~~
Prove you're real!

She still thinks I'm a figment of her imagination, and I'm okay with that—I *was* okay with that—but if she truly wants to meet the man behind the mask, her Phantom, then I'll show her just how real I am.

Chapter Five

My visit with Holden replays in my mind.

I am *not* a little doe, but something about being under his massive form, like a doe beneath a lion's salivating teeth, ready to tear into dinner, left my stomach fluttering with confusion.

I can't let myself think this way. I've trained for too long to let a few brash words pull my focus away from killing his brother.

My father always said it's easy to open a door but wiser to have someone else do it for you. I don't share that same sentiment in this situation. I need to be the one to kill Silas, but that doesn't mean I can't find a way to use Holden in some way to accomplish my task.

I know a few ways we can use him...

Stop it!

"Suck it in a little more." Aspen pulls the laces tighter around my ribs. She offered her own services in place of my maid to get to know me better, her future sister-in-law, which starts with teaching me how to dress like them despite my repeated insistence not to.

We bickered back and forth until finally settling on the corset dress, and only because it's black with a lace trimming that I couldn't resist wearing. However, I absolutely refused the ridiculous, wired skirt, and bows.

My hair is braided into a tight bun on top of my head to conceal the small dagger I keep with me at all times. A few loose pieces hang around my temples at Aspen's request, insisting it looks more 'beautiful and romantic.' My ruby choker stays as it always does, tight around my neck with the matching black velvet cuffs around my wrists.

I suck in a deep breath and brace my hands around the bedpost while Aspen pulls the laces tighter, humming a soft melody. "Little bites tonight, and I'll ensure the leftovers are brought to your room, so you can feed properly later."

Maison snorts in the corner with a shake of his head. His slicked-back, wavy blonde hair was too similar to Silas' perfect, put-together appearance, so I gave him a quick trim and parted it, leaving a loose piece to fall over his brow. "Feed? Like a pig at a trough?" His grin heightens, and I already know what he's going to say before he does. "I suppose you do eat like one."

Ignoring him, I turn my question to Aspen. "You do this every day?" My ribs are screaming with agony already, threatening to crack under the pressure. How I am going to sit is a question for later.

Aspen nods and smiles sweetly. This is a different side of the girl I met earlier. Her face is clean, her blood-red lips are gone, and the red bow perfectly wrapped on top of her head gives her a more innocent and friendly appearance, a young girl rather than someone in her early twenties. The puffed sleeves and high neckline of the royal blue and white dress give her a childish look that I don't envy.

"You'll get used to it. You'll only need these for special occasions like balls, or having guests over for dinners, or when you're entertaining."

Hopefully this will all be over before any of that happens. The prince's death date is growing closer by the minute if I'm required to wear this regularly.

It's moments like this that I'm thankful my father never cared about frivolous things such as ensuring our corsets were tied tight. Maybe if we had a mother things would be different, but she died when we were all too young to remember her.

"I recommend wearing less makeup. The king doesn't favor the look of…" She pauses to observe me closer. "Your makeup is scandalous. It makes you look older and off-putting. Like a harlot." That explains her missing red lipstick but doesn't explain why she wore it in the first place. Then again, I know all about wanting to grow up and having a father who refuses to see me as anything other than… my mind blanks at the thought.

Because father prefers Mel. We're the damaged one.

I don't disagree with the voices this time. I would wager he didn't notice my disappearance until Mel brought it to his attention.

From the corner of my eye, I notice Maison side-eying Aspen with a curl in his lip and his hand wrapped around the hilt of his sword. He doesn't take kindly to anyone who so much as looks at me with a crease in their brows, let alone openly tries to insult me—unless it's him.

I'm not offended by Aspen's observations in the slightest. My sister-in-law was a harlot and is one of the sweetest women I've ever met. I wish I had her experience. She's confident and knows exactly what to say to wrangle my brother in. He's hypnotized every time she's in the same room as him. If I had that kind of power over Silas, it would be easy to kill him.

It was easy. You had the knife at his throat and still couldn't do it.

We're no longer discussing that.

Although I am starting to think my voice has the right idea and Holden can help me in more ways than I first anticipated.

"Like the necklace and cuffs, it's non-negotiable." I don't look away, so she knows just how serious I am.

"Can I ask why?"

I make the effort to soften my face at the sight of her reddened cheeks. Either she has a crush on me or I'm making her nervous for a reason I am unaware of. "I'll tell you why if you tell me something in return." Another trick from my father: never offer anything up without receiving something in return, preferably something of more value.

Aspen nods.

"What is the deal with your brothers? Do they get along? Do they… have lovers?"

I can hear Maison's eye roll.

Aspen doesn't appear taken aback by the question, if anything, she looks like she expected something on the topic with the way she attempts to hide her smile by biting the inside of her lip. Or maybe it's to keep them from singing a song she doesn't want to let slip.

"They have many lovers. Women throw themselves at them." Her round face twists with disgust. "It's appalling. No offense."

She flings the sheet off the mirror to examine herself, her eyes narrowing on me when I jump out of the way to avoid my reflection. "You know Silas' reputation," she continues, "I can't tell you too much beyond that. Why you chose to marry him anyway is why I wanted to get to know you better. To see how mental you are for such a decision."

Her choice of words makes me too aware of the smile I'm planting on my face to appear polite. I swear I can see where the bed lumps from the diary tucked beneath it.

"Silas does everything to be the perfect heir," she goes on, looking over each book spine lined along the vanity, "but he still can't gain our father's approval, so he acts out by disappearing for days on end, which my father hates because Holden does the same. As for Holden, he hunts. There's not much more to him than that." She spins around, her hands resting on the edge as she takes me in with a smile that tells me she's enjoying having my ear. "They do get along in one instance and one instance only, but I doubt you'll stay here long enough to see that."

When she doesn't explain, I ask her to tell me, acutely aware of her last statement and the softness of her that almost drowned it out.

"When they have a woman naked between them."

A heated flush rises to my cheeks. How she knows this information is something I don't want to press further for.

Noting her raised brow, I remember I'm supposed to tell her about the necklace and bracelets. "The jewelry hides my scars. And the makeup," I contemplate lying, but there is no harm in telling her the truth. "It makes me comfortable in public."

My answer seems to please her. A soft smile graces her angelic face as she leans closer, her lips next to my ear. "Be careful what you say aloud, even in your room. There's always someone listening."

I let her leave first, telling her I'll catch up after I use the washroom.

"Absolute cunt." Maison doubles down on his first observation of her once the door shuts, holding out my tube of red lipstick. "I would never swear in front of a lady, but considering you look like a harlot," he teases, giving me his sheepish grin while I apply a thick layer on my lips. "Fuck that girl. I hope she chokes while watching you eat an entire steak."

"If we're lucky, Silas will too."

I rush to my bed, pull the diary out of its hiding place, and flip to the newest entry. Anticipation causes me to fumble through the pages until I find what I'm looking for. Next to pressed violas is my Phantom's reply:

*I've never tasted anything so **otherworldly**, so divine as you. If you thought you'd never experience me again, you're wrong, little Reaper. You came to me this time, and I'm no longer settling for watching you try to recreate what only I can give you.*
Pink book, page 56—Tonight.

The dining room tables are set in a circle, allowing everyone a view of each guest. The decorations are simple and not as excessive as most royals. Tapestries of the forest and paintings of the Whitehart family hang throughout the great hall, with candelabras lighting a butterscotch hue around the room, threatening to set the art aflame with the right gust of wind.

The room is already full of conversation as servants walk around with trays of champagne, wine, whisky, and scotch. Others, the more interesting servants, carry bite-sized appetizers my fingers itch to grab.

FATEFUL CHANCE

Maison and my grumpy guard stand by the door with Aspen's other six, who dwarf in comparison, all looking like perfect statues, though each of them has their quirks that set them apart. There's the one with the big eyes that find my chest more often than not, the one with the glasses, the one with the red cheeks, one who clearly drinks too much with the way his eyes droop and is identical to the one who's yawning, and the last one who gives me a smile and a wink, much too happy for my liking.

The one Aspen gifted me is off-putting; his chiseled jaw never moves to smile or talk, his brows are set in a way that makes him look angry, and when he looks at me, I can see him calculating ways he can rid himself of having to watch me. It's strange for such a young guard to be so stoic and pissed off. They typically hold a lightness in them, an eagerness that gets wiped away *after* years of service.

Or maybe he's just phenomenal at his job. I would have thought twice before entering Silas' room if this man were standing guard, unlike Maison, who has the same taut muscular build that's threatening enough to anyone who thinks about approaching him, but holds a softness in his face that's trusting.

"You okay?" Aspen asks, following my gaze to the guards.

I nod, but she's handing me a drink and skipping toward Holden before I can verbally answer.

Part of me sinks into myself at the swift dismissal, but I recover quickly, grabbing at the passing trays to fill my hands with different bite-sized appetizers. Once I do, I perch myself against the wall to observe everyone at once, which is hard when I can't keep my glances from Holden and Aspen. There's a tenderness in the way he looks at her. I wouldn't have expected such a brute of a man to possess such affection.

I tear myself from the siblings to look around the rest of the crowded room, noticing most of the faces from other balls I've attended over the past year. Everyone has been making the same annual rounds: princesses positioning themselves for princes, kings declaring their intentions for potential alliances, and princes usually sneaking off to consort with women they wouldn't be required to marry.

Silas and Holden are the same as the rest, I remind myself. And yet I found Silas napping in his room the night of the ball.

His mistress must have left earlier or was to come later. Now that I think of it, it had been a mistake not to take that into account. The rat, whoever it was, insisted Silas often spent time alone in his room, both with and without concubines, but ensured that night he wouldn't be with one.

At the thought, I find Silas with his princely smile, his back straighter than the wall itself, a scotch in his hand. He speaks with his father and another man I recognize as the Sea King.

My father won't like that. He's been trying to get into King Tydas' good graces for years, but the man is shut off from making any further alliances. Too untrusting with their kingdom words: *Loyal and proud; with voices so loud, they'll have more than your feet bound.*

Maybe this marriage could be useful in multiple ways: bind myself to the prince with this marriage and secure my father with King Tydas' alliance.

One task at a time.

On a positive note, multitasking is fun and gets more done.

I snag another breaded bite with a creamy sauce that makes my eyes roll back.

"It's good, but I have to say you make that look a lot better than it is." A familiar voice tickles my ear. I turn to see Holden with that lazy grin, his hands behind his back. How did I not see or hear him approach?

"It's fantastic," I say with the bread still melting in my mouth. "Sorry." I finish swallowing, then grab a glass of champagne, regrettably, to wash it down faster.

"No need to apologize," he assures, looking more princely than brute in his formal attire that closely resembles Silas, although no one could look as perfect as the Damned Prince. His chocolate hair is brushed back, his posture is straight, and his smile is symmetrical with his perfect white teeth on display. He holds himself with a strength and confidence that's exactly how the heir should present himself.

A wolf in prince clothing. A monster hiding in plain sight.

By the looks of it, King Tydas eyes him with the same acute assessment I'm giving him. I don't remember him looking so...

Hazel eyes meet mine just as Holden steps into my line of vision, cutting me off before I can make a fool of myself and drool over the beautiful bastard. My stomach twists with punishing nausea at the thought of thinking of him so kindly.

"I'll make sure the kitchen staff sends that appetizer to your room every night, so long as I'm invited to join you."

I cough into my glass. "That seems inappropriate, considering I'm engaged to your brother."

"For lessons, of course. You're obviously better at playing with daggers than I am, and I am willing to admit I could learn a few things, even if it is from a woman." He winks. There's no ignoring the heat that pools low in my stomach at the sight. "I can show you a few things, too."

I knew it.

"A woman who's won awards for her dagger throwing." Silas stands beside me, eyeing his brother with what I could only describe as a promising threat while still wearing that fake, perfect smile.

Impressive. Maybe he can show us a few things, too.

Stop it.

With both of them so close, I can see the resemblance. They share the same dark hair, though Silas' is shorter and kept sleeked back, whereas Holden's is longer and tied at the nape of his neck. Holden is taller and stockier, but they share the same cut, muscular stature that comes with daily training, and their grins are nearly identical, except Silas' is the fake princely one that holds threats his lips won't speak where Holden's comes with a playful slyness I'm familiar with.

"I wouldn't underestimate the evil little princess," Silas places his hand on the curve of my back. Anyone looking would see it as a loving gesture, but I can feel the stake being made, claiming me as his in front of his brother and anyone else who dares approach me with the same flirty interest. "She didn't get the name Vulture for her curtsy."

Both cursed names given to me, evil and Vulture, have my skin prickling.

I am not evil.

I step out of his touch, making a show of grabbing another drink from a passing tray, realizing I now have two full ones with nowhere to put them. "How do you know I won awards?"

Silas tosses the rest of his drink back and places it on another passing tray, taking one of my flutes for himself. "You don't think I know who

I'm engaged to?" For some reason, it feels like there is more meaning there, but I don't get time to dissect it before his proposition. "Why don't you show my brother how skilled you are? Are you familiar with finger roulette?"

"Are you offering up your precious fingers?" I cock my brow.

He wiggles them in the air. "I'm all yours, evil princess."

Rather than expose where I keep the blades riddled over the various parts of my body, I step into him. Our chests are a millimeter apart as I slither my hands down his waist. I expect him to be too caught off guard and step away, but the asshole grabs mine right back to pull me flush against him.

His crooked grin has me grabbing the dagger tucked at his hip with more urgency, before I can acknowledge how firm he is.

"Take a seat," I order.

We make our way to the seats, away from the crowd, and at the annoyance of the servants trying to set the tables. Holden takes the seat next to me while Silas spins a chair around the table across from us. Before he can get comfortable, I lift his chin with the tip of his blade, dragging his eyes from my corset to mine. The open threat brings us right back to the familiar tension in his room. "Let's make this interesting," I tilt my head with a thought. "If I don't slip in ten rounds, you give me back my knife."

"And if you do slip?" He gently grabs my wrist to lower the pointed steel from his neck.

Holden barks a laugh. "That's boring. If you stab him, you sleep in the old mining tunnels for the night."

That's one question answered. The secret door in the basement does lead to the old mining tunnels.

"And if I don't?" There isn't a chance I will.

"Take that necklace off," Holden suggests.

"No!" My objection turns a few heads. I clutch the ruby around my neck just to ensure it's still tight and secure.

"Dance with me." Our attention snaps to Silas.

"I don't dance." I'll never dance again if I have a say in it.

"You will if you don't stab me, unless you want to sleep in the old mining tunnels."

They're enjoying this a little too much, both with their wolfish grins. I can't argue against them unless I want them to think I have doubt in my ability to win this game.

No, I won't give them the satisfaction.

I sigh with all the annoyance I feel. "I thought I was supposed to get something out of this."

Holden snickers.

Silas flares his hand. "Eyes on me, princess."

I twirl the dagger and stab the tip softly next to his thumb, lift and bring it down between the first finger, then the next, and the next, over and over again. My eyes remain glued on Silas' with every sharp motion.

FATEFUL CHANCE

My breath is held hostage in my lungs while my mind fights with itself. I could stab him on purpose, but my pride would be wounded right next to his hand.

I'm seven rounds in, eight, nine...

There isn't anything outside of his hand and my dagger. Not the curl in his mouth, the crinkle smile in his eyes, or the heavy presence of Holden at my side, *nothing* can draw me away from my deadly focus.

I'm on the tenth and final round when a servant shouts that dinner is served. The knife slips at the last second, but Silas doesn't flinch. His steady hold and confidence sway me to angle the knife perfectly flush with his skin.

My eyes widen, unblinking. All air in my lungs is stolen, waiting for the crimson that doesn't come. The relief I feel when he pulls his hand away, revealing no blood or scratch, rushes through me with a high that I live for.

Holden clasps my back in the way men do when they're impressed. "Like I said, I'll happily take lessons from you."

Silas pulls his chair back around, caging me directly between them. "Not bad, princess."

Adrenaline is still surging through me during dinner. The King announces the engagement to the applause and praise of everyone in the dining circle. Champagne is poured while the five courses are served. I dissociate from it all, placing a smile on my face for everyone to look at while I secretly plan and map possible scenarios of killing the man on my left by using the help of the man on my right.

In the end, I'm thinking about the Phantom and how I need this dinner to be over so I can get back to my chambers to read the passage he instructed me to. If he's real... I scan the room and shake that thought away. He'd have to be someone within my own court.

Aspen, on the other side of Holden, leans forward to give me a cautious glare as I take a third bite of steak. I don't need the reminder when my ribs are on the verge of cracking and my breath is shortening by the second. I sit taller to relieve the pressure, but all that does is allow the ties to find a new angle to slowly torture me.

A sharp inhale takes me by surprise when something hits my right knee—Holden. The back of his head is to me while he speaks with a man I don't recognize, without a hint that he's sent my skin ablaze.

No man has touched me like this. Men favor my sister, the *fun* one, not me.

I suck in another breath as a tighter grip wraps around my left thigh. Silas glances at his brother's hand and smirks, leaning in with a whisper that tickles my ear. "Are you working on bedding *two* princes, evil princess?"

"I hear you two like to share," I retort.

His eyes narrow. "Is that what you want? Both Whitehart brothers warming your bed?"

"I do just fine warming my bed myself."

His lips curve even higher. "You're a horrible liar." His grip tightens on my knee at the same moment his brother's does. They're so in sync that I don't have a single doubt that they've done this before.

I'm just a game to them. Some girl they think they can get between them for a night of debauchery, one of their conquests they can laugh and talk about later.

My cheeks flare with a heat that bursts through me. I have too vivid of an imagination to linger on those thoughts at the dining table.

Pushing them away isn't an option. It would only bring more attention that I don't want or need on me. As impossible as it is with being engaged to the Whitehart heir, the Damned Prince no one ever thought would marry, I want to go as unnoticed as possible here.

Silas ignores his whiskey to sip his water, leaning in to whisper again. "I'd wager you spent too much time training with those daggers to enjoy yourself, haven't you?"

I don't answer because I'm not entirely sure what the question is. I enjoy myself just fine.

Liar. We're so boring.

I don't notice his other hand reaching over until his fingers brush the ruby at my neck.

"If I promise you can be the death of me, will you let me enjoy you a little first?"

Oh.

A sharp inhale is all I can take with the tightening corset. "First, you tried to kill me. Now you want to…"

My ears scratch at the sound of a sharp crunch on my other side. While any distraction from Silas is appreciated, my stomach sours at the sound of *that* specific crunch.

I spin my head around, taking in what little gasp my corset allows. Holden stabs a sliver of a bright green apple with his fork, his teeth coming down on the tarty fruit again.

Silas pulls my chin back to him, looking down at me with a strange expression my vision can't fully take in with the black spots that appear around me.

I need to get out of here.

Without being able to speak to excuse myself, I rush out of the room. Every step is a struggle, but I need to get away before I cause a scene. Maison and my new guard follow without a word.

The door clicks shut. My knees fall to the hard floor.

Fucking thrones, I internally curse as pain shoots up my legs.

My vision tunnels with every shallow breath. My fingers can't grasp the strings behind my back to loosen the corset.

Help! I want to scream but I can't while sucking in as much air as I can.

I turn and fall on my back, seeing both guards a few feet away, tilting their heads in confusion.

"Eva!" I hear someone shout, but my ears are filled with a pounding that drowns out their voice.

It feels like my head is wrapped in that sack again, plunging me back into the darkness I escaped. My hands fly to my face with real panic, but I can't sigh in relief when I feel my skin instead of burlap because there is no breath left in me.

Blurry black stars fall down the ceiling until all I see is black.

Crack!

My ribs must be breaking.

FATEFUL CHANCE

Something sharp taps my chest. The relief in my torso isn't painless, if anything, it makes me want to scream out, but I'm too busy sucking down air to keep me from dying.

A cold chill kisses my flesh.

That can't be right.

I drop my hands to my chest. Sure enough, my breasts are out, my nipples pebbled. As something warm is placed over me, I'm lifted up like the bride I'm soon to be.

I want to protest that I can walk by myself, but I'm too tired and in too much pain to care who is helping me.

Soon enough, I hear a door kick open, and I'm placed on top of a warm bed in a dark room.

"Your corset was too tight. I had to cut it off." I'm positive that's Silas' voice, but I don't know why he'd help me.

I lift my head, but my shoulders are pushed back down.

I don't know if he leaves before sleep takes over, but when I open my eyes, it's not Silas looming over me.

Draped in shadows, his head tilts like a villain out of a horror novel as his hand collars my neck.

Phantom

Eva's soft breaths filter through the dark shadows, her brows creasing in whatever nightmare is starting to plague her. She's been asleep for a few hours, spiraling into the hell inside her mind for the last ten minutes: whimpering, whispering, tossing and turning her head.

Lowering the blankets, I see she's still naked, her small body splayed out like a sacrificial offering. Her tear-shaped breasts are begging for my touch. All of her is begging for me. I can feel the ache in her like I feel it in myself.

My fingers graze over her, starting at the valley between her breasts and trailing past her navel. I find that wet spot between her legs. My blood heats. Eva's body has always responded to mine, even when she's not aware of it, *especially* when she's not aware of it.

Seeing her struggling at dinner was the highlight of my day. Not when she was knocking on death's door, that's a horror I never wish to experience again. She's only allowed to be on the cusp of dying under my hands, and only so I can bring her back.

No, it was her elated glow after playing finger roulette, when her fair cheeks flushed with the undeniable guilty lust at having two men literally grabbing for her attention. My sheltered, little Reaper likes to be fawned over, wanted, and craved.

Her groan has my head jerking away from the apex of her thighs. Her eyes flutter open. Naturally, my fingers find her neck, feeling her steady pulse quickening.

She writes about the voices in her head giving sexual innuendos at the most inconvenient times, and those internal arguments were written all over her face during dinner, just like they are at this very moment.

"You…" Her voice is soft and ragged from struggling for air. "I knew you were real."

"No, you didn't," she immediately answers herself.

I've read about her episodes, but witnessing it first-hand is something else—chilling. She fits this manor better than I ever imagined, and I've imagined it quite a bit over the years.

Tilting my head, I study her, finding her lips moving with whatever debate she's having in that pretty head of hers. She's too distracted to realize she's naked, and I'm too drawn to the flush creeping up her neck and filling her cheeks to let her know.

"Did you read the book?"

Her brows pinch before offering a silent no. This is the first time she's ever consciously heard me speak, not in my own voice, of course, but I can see her straining to place it.

She watches my every move as I pull the book from behind my back and flip to the page I want:

My arms are too heavy, my breasts too full as his tongue slides up and down my——

"What are you reading?!" She shifts her back against the headboard, quickly pulling the duvet to cover herself. The dip between her collarbone sinks with the breaths she's trying to steady.

"Are you scared of me, little Reaper?" She is. Not because I might kill her, but because I might not be real. I take a step closer, letting my presence overcome her.

"You've never hurt me," she answers with an undeniable thickening in her voice, followed by "*yet.*"

I start again:

...center, as his fingers press into me. I can't hold myself up much longer, but I'm so close. The way he fills me...

I shift my eyes to her. Her lips are parted. Her hands clutch the comforter like a lifeline, leaving the sight of her cleavage to taunt me. Cleavage Aspen's guards couldn't stop staring at. They'll learn soon enough to keep their eyes to themselves.

"Why..." Her throat bobs with a silent gulp. "Why did you stop?"

She can't see it, but the smile on my face has never been higher. She's been waiting for me to come back and make her dance between the veils again, but I haven't let myself. I knew if I had another taste, I'd become addicted and never let her go, never let her marry the prince she was supposed to, have little heirs, and live that perfect, happy life she used to dream of. Only my hands and fingers have done what she needed, until now.

"Do you remember your word?"

Her head's moving before she has a chance to use her voice.

"Tell me." It takes effort to stay still while watching her throat bob and lips part to say the one word that lets me know she wants me to stop. With her past, she needed an out, a sense of safety and control, even though she's never had either with me.

"Coffin."

She's only used that word twice. The first to tell me what word she wanted, and now, telling me she remembers it. Fitting that we'll both end up in one if she actually uses it.

I lower so we're a breath apart, her eyes flaring at the sudden closeness, working to figure out if this is real. My knuckles graze her neck again, shifting to feel that hard pattering against my palm. "Get on your knees and grab the bedpost."

"Ask him." She bites her lip, realizing she spoke the thought out loud. "Who are you?"

I let out a deep laugh that's cut short when I see her reaching for the dagger on the side table. "I believe you call me your Phantom. And you're my little Reaper. We don't have to be anyone else tonight."

As much as I love hearing her snarky ass remarks, seeing her speechless and all-around vulnerable beneath me is just as intoxicating. "What are you going to do to me?"

"Whatever I want." I lean down and pull the braid from atop her head, slowly unraveling it strand by strand until her black locks cascade over her shoulders. The blade she keeps there tumbles onto the carpet. Her pupils suffocate all the viridian in her eyes.

"Now," I brush my thumb across her bottom lip. "Are you going to be a good girl and do as I say?"

"Absolutely… *shut up*… but he's so…" It's cute watching her argue with herself, but my time is limited, and I don't have all night to let her process what's real or not.

Taking the covers from her grip, I lower them just enough to expose her breasts again. I drag my knuckles along her collarbone, testing her reaction.

Unconsciously, she withers and groans. Consciously, her eyes lift to the slits in my mask, trying to see the person behind it. Her lips move again, but my attention is pulled to the rise and fall of her chest as I trail my fingers until I'm cupping her breasts. They fit so perfectly in my palm.

My thumb brushes over her nipple and her head falls back with the softest sigh.

"*Knees*," I order, rolling both nipples between my fingers. "Bedpost."

She doesn't argue as she crawls to her knees and places her hands around the wooden bedpost, unaware that this isn't her room.

Her small, naked body is the shade of bone, iridescent in the darkness, making her appear like one of the spirits that are said to haunt this place. Her hair trails to the tip of her ass where the arch in her back gives me the perfect view of her heart-shaped cheeks. The way she grabs the necklace around her neck like it's an old relic as she peeks back at me is the most hauntingly beautiful image I've ever seen.

If I were skilled with paint and a brush, I'd make her stay in this position so I could capture it forever.

But again, I don't have all night.

Lifting myself onto the bed, I come behind her to push her knees farther apart, telling her to stay still before flipping onto my back.

Wrapping my arms around her legs, I lift the mask enough to lower her onto my tongue.

Her hips jerk, but I hold her in place, dragging my tongue up and down her center until her writhing melts.

I bury my tongue in her and she tastes like addiction—sweet, raw, and fucking divine—like any vice would never be enough to stave off my need for the next hit.

This is why I stayed away.

It's her surrender, the way she lets go of every thought in her head, drops every wall, releases every guard—that impenetrable castle that is Eva crumbles away completely when I'm between her legs.

I drag my tongue to tease her clit, repeating the same motions.

"Bleeding thrones... I..." Her legs start to shake. Her pulse beats against my ear where it presses on her thigh.

That mouth on her has mine slowing to draw this out as long as possible. "Is this real enough for you?"

I slide my hands up the back of her thighs and around her ass, pulling her down on me harder while sucking that little nub into my mouth, rolling it along my tongue.

There isn't a sweeter taste or a more erotic sight than her sitting on my face, her hips grinding, riding my tongue at her own pace with my hands to keep her steady.

Tugging on her hair, I pull her head toward me. My hand wraps around her throat. Her eyes widen, but she doesn't back away.

"Let go, little Reaper." I squeeze, slowly. "Let me hold you between this world and the next."

She once wrote that she thinks of death daily, that every time she does, she's reminded of the horrors of her past. I'm not letting that plague her anymore. Now, when she thinks of death, she'll only think of me, the Phantom that brings her toward it but never lets her cross over completely.

Her savior.

Her breath stutters, her pulse hammering beneath my palm, desperate for more air as she continues to ride my face with less control. She grips my wrist, the one that's controlling her life.

When she shudders above me, when her cheeks are a rosy pink, I let go. "Come back to me, little Reaper." Her gasps fill with an unholy moan as her hips continue to grind against me.

My cock throbs to taste her, but I won't give in yet. Not until I have her undivided attention, and right now, she has too many men pulling for it. By the time I'm done with her, she'll be too consumed by me to notice anyone else.

Chapter Six

My eyes aren't even open before the deep ache in my ribs leaves me huffing into the overly fluffed pillow that smells of leather, vanilla, and a soft hint of the floral soaps I found in my washroom.

Memories of last night hit me one after another: the passing trays, finger roulette, eating, trying to breathe, Holden and Silas touching me...

I lower the duvet, finding hints that my last memory—*or hallucination*—might have been real, considering I'm stark naked.

My Phantom was here.

I find my neck, my ruby firmly in place. I can still feel his hands wrapped around it, a tether, holding me between the veils while he took my breath and then gave it back to me.

There are no words to describe the rush of having someone hold your life in their hands, of inching closer to death's kiss, but knowing they won't let you cross that line.

But then again, what are the odds that my breath was taken twice? Once by the corset and again by my Phantom? My mind works to right itself all the time, making excuses or romanticizing situations and memories to make them less traumatic and more enjoyable.

It was enjoyable.

We're sick. No one should want to ride death so closely.

If he's death, I want to ride him all the time, actually.

I jump out of bed, but when I reach for my diary, it's gone. I snap my search to the vanity, but it's not there either. I'm not in my room at all. The familiar midnight blue covers, the neat desk with too many books, the chessboard, the half-melted tapered candles, the roaring fireplace, and somber art that depicts nothing but somehow ruminates melancholy with their muted colors, sharp, drastic edges, and soft, wistful blends. Silas' room is a conundrum I want nothing to do with.

My feet sway beneath me at the sharp disappointment that rips through me. If I'm not in my room, then the Phantom must have been a dream. I would have noticed sitting on his face on the same bed I attempted to slit the prince's throat.

It shouldn't disappoint or surprise me, but as I slip into the lilac nightgown left on the bedpost, I simmer with more embarrassment than rage. I hate myself. I hate that I'm delusional and somehow found myself naked in my enemy's bed, having a sex dream about someone who doesn't exist.

Why couldn't it have been Holden's bed? At least then... I shake the thought away. Holden doesn't seem the type to simply drop a girl into his bed and leave, which would only complicate this situation further.

I'm chalking it up to the lack of oxygen from the corset. That's the only explanation for this mess. That and the lack of dinner have clearly left me starved for more than food. Something I need to remedy before I do something I regret, or worse, get myself killed.

The nightgown clings to me like a second layer of skin as I make my way down the dark hallway.

Creeeeak!

I twist back. There's nothing but the long lane of closed doors and the soft sconces flickering the shadows into a dark dance with the light, giving this manor that dull and ominous energy it's known for.

Not even my grumpy guard is in sight. *Useless twat.*

My stomach groans. A warning to anyone behind me that I'm starving and likely to chew their head off if they so much as think about attacking me before I eat.

When I turn back, my face bounces off a hard chest. "Long night for you, wasn't it?" Maison grins ear to ear.

I smack his shoulder and scold him for letting Silas drag me to his room overnight, demanding he tell me where he was and why he didn't carry me back to my own bed.

He shrugs, his hands clasping behind his back. "It sounded like you didn't want to be bothered, and as I've been saying for years, you need a little tension release. Although," his fingers dig into my shoulders, "you did a terrible job."

"You're one to talk!" I flick my family crest that's pinned over the heart of his leather armor. "The most action you get is watching me walk to the washroom."

"Do you think that I would tell a princess of my nightly escapades?"

I snort at his wry grin. He's handsome, royally so. His strong jaw and trusting eyes, paired with his solid form and sarcastic sense of humor, would lure any woman to bed. I'd never inflate his ego and tell him that though.

"I already know them. You stand ten feet away and wait until I wake up to entertain you." My face falls thinking about last night. "Did you…" Heat rushes to my cheeks as I stumble on the question I *need* answered. "Did you happen to see or hear anyone else?"

His brows lift with concern.

"Where's Digby?" A harsh voice brings both of our heads swiveling back down the haunting hallway. The grumpy guard's hand is at his hilt, scanning us and the rest of our empty surroundings.

"Who?" I ask.

"The dumb one, big eyes, stares at your tits. I'm back to relieve him."

I shake my head and tell him he's the only dumb one I've seen today, and that if he needs me, he can find me in the kitchens. Maison humors me with a quick laugh while the grumpy one gives me a dismissive eye roll before posting himself in front of my door.

I turn back to my task at hand and head toward the kitchens, leaving both guards behind.

The labyrinth that makes up the manor isn't hard to navigate. I studied the maps for months, ensuring I knew precisely where the kitchens were in relation to nearly every room—the heart of every home.

When I'm close enough to smell the remnants of what must have been a strawberry pie and something chocolate for dessert, I pause with my hand over the doorknob. A faint rustling comes from behind it, too quiet to be the servants cleaning up.

Gently, I push on the edge of the door, trying not to disturb whoever is on the other side too abruptly. The sight that welcomes me is the last thing I expected to see.

Silas is shirtless. His firm pecs shift with each circular whisk around the ceramic bowl while humming a soft melody with his eyes closed. Some of the golden batter spills over the side and plops onto the counter.

Without dropping the bowl, he cracks in an egg before working the whisk again, turns to the stove, and whisks something simmering in a pot. His movements are so fluid and precise, he must do this often.

This is my chance. He is all alone in the kitchen. No one would see me kill him. With his back turned, not even he would see it. I could make it look like a cooking accident gone wrong.

But if I kill him now, I won't get a chance at an alliance with King Tydas.

My arguments, all thoughts, and plans wither away when I realize what I'm looking at. Long, angry scars lash across Silas' back: deep, raised, red, and white, long, short, jagged, thin, and thick... The brutality beaten into his hard muscles with the juxtaposition of him holding batter reminds me of the paintings on his walls.

He turns around, and the smallest smile lifts as he leans back against the counter and continues whisking the bowl wrapped within the crook of his arm. He couldn't get rid of his perfect posture if he tried, but he looks different, more relaxed. His shoulders aren't as tense as they usually are. His face is softer, and his jaw isn't so rigid. There is no questioning threat lingering behind the fake mask he sets for the world.

The vicious wolf hidden beneath is tamer than I expected.

He stops whisking to toss something I can't see into his mouth, wiping away the red that slips down the side of his lip. His tongue jumps out to clean off his finger.

My lower stomach flutters with the memory of last night. My phantom's fingers and tongue…

His body stiffens, tensing back to the stone I'm sure he was built of. His eyes lift, landing directly on me. Part of me is tickled seeing them widen a bit from being caught off guard.

"You're horrible at sneaking around." Genuine amusement fills his voice.

I swallow my pride and let the door slam behind me, knowing full well there is no hiding the blush that is surely staining my cheeks. I have been caught openly gawking at this man three times now.

"You don't even know how long I was there." I bit my lip, internally cringing. I'm painting myself to sound like a stalker. "You have to be the messiest baker I've ever—"

"*Watched intently*," he finishes with a smirk.

I cross my arms. "I was just coming by for some leftovers."

"I work up an appetite after so much rest, too. And you do look *well* rested."

My lips pinch at whatever he's insinuating when it hits me; I was in *his* bed. What if I touched myself while dreaming of the Phantom? It wouldn't be the first time. What if he heard whatever Maison heard last night? I swallow those heated worries deep, *deep* down. "Now that all the oxygen is back into my body, I'm hungry."

"The words you're looking for are *thank* and *you*. If you care to elaborate, you can add *for saving my life*. And if you really want to go the extra mile, please do add, *my handsome prince*."

My sights shift to the knife lying on the granite counter between us. Silas tracks the movement and quickly tosses it in the sink behind him. "Really? Even after I saved you? Can I at least know why you're relentless in wanting to kill me?"

"You know why." My voice is too low and tight to sound at all intimidating.

Dragging his hand over his naked heart, he looks at me with a visible softness, all evidence of his usual arrogance gone. "I swear it on everything I own and love, I sincerely have no idea why you, Evangeline, my evil little princess, would want to kill me."

"You must not own or love anything then," I say. "And I'm not your little anything."

He eats the distance between us in two steps, lifting my chin with the tip of his finger. The touch alone nearly knocks me off my feet while my neck cranes back, too trapped in whatever lure those hazels possess.

Gods, he is tall. My heightened chin barely meets his shoulders. "You're my *everything*. Or have you forgotten you're my fiancé?"

My focus falls to the pad of his thumb brushing my skin. It was only a few hours ago that these same fingers were cutting my corset clean off me. A few hours since those caramel eyes saw what that corset kept tight in place, possibly pleasuring myself in *his* bed.

His gaze falls to where his thumb moves to caress my bottom lip. "Do you understand?" His head cocks to the side. "On second thought, I think it's best I make myself a little more clear."

My stomach pulls lower, heating every inch of me, warning me to back away, to run to the knife and stab this man like I was supposed to. But I'm stuck. It's as if I'm made of metal, and he continues to set me on fire, welding my entire being in place whenever he's around.

Our lips are so close I can smell the strawberries on his breath.

When they brush mine, it takes everything in me to pull myself away. "If you consider me your everything, can we start with customer, because like I said, I'm hungry."

I make my way to the other side of the counter, as far away from him as the kitchen allows, ignoring that pull toward the knife. At this point, it would be stupid to try to kill him when he is acutely aware of my plans and watches my every move. I need to see it as the sign that it is and wait until after the wedding. I'll secure Whitehart and King Tydas' alliance for my father while also being a widow and never expected to marry again. What is the phrase? Two birds, one stone, or in this case, three birds, one dagger.

"What are you making anyway?" I eye the mess, the eight bowls, three pans, spilled batter, and endless whisks cluttered along every surface.

"Cookies, brownies, strawberry pie," he answers, tossing me a brownie before going back to whisking his bowl. He isn't as relaxed as he was when he thought he was alone, but he also isn't the statue he is when others are around, particularly his father.

I spot where one scar comes to the top of his shoulders and wonder if it was King Byron who mutilated him—his own son. If so, our fathers are far more alike than I thought. *We* are more alike than I care to admit.

"For what?" I press, both baffled that a prince could cook anything and intrigued as to the reason for the excessive amount.

FATEFUL CHANCE

My stomach makes its thoughts on the chocolate square known with a loud groan, begging to dismiss the fact that it could be poisoned so long as it's satiating. Besides my father, my hunger is the only other thing I can never deny.

I take a bite and the world stops. The thick brown treat melts in my mouth, and I haven't even had a chance to chew it. Every movement on my tongue is an experience I never want to end.

The sound of a whisk hitting the ceramic bowl stalls. When I open my eyes, I find him studying me. "I want to enjoy food as much as you do."

"When you starve for a year, you learn to enjoy it." My throat tightens at the accidental confession. Then again, he was the one to starve me, so why does he look like he pities me right now? I swallow the growing thickness. "What happened to your back?"

The bowl slides across the counter, spilling over the sides by the time it stops perfectly in front of me. "I'll tell you how I got my scars if you tell me why you want to kill me, but since I know you won't be doing that, you might as well help."

Plopping the rest of the chocolate in my mouth, I grab the whisk and begin to stir the batter that is far too runny. I'm not going to give him the satisfaction of hearing me talk about the torture he put me through.

"This has too many eggs." I round the counter and grab the flour next to him at the exact moment he does, sending white powder into the air. Right into our faces.

"Silas!" I yell, wiping my face.

"Oops." He laughs. "I didn't see you."

CRUEL KINGDOMS

I fist a handful of flour and toss it at him, coating his face and shoulders. We both eye the eggs on the counter. I'm faster. Grabbing two at a time, I toss one, hitting his chest. The other, he ducks before it can hit his forehead, but he already has four ready to go.

I turn, but he's too fast. My arm yanks back, bringing my back flush against him. Eggs crack against my collarbone and shoulder.

Huffing, I tear myself away and grab the bag of sugar, dumping it over his head. I don't get one step back before he's grabbing the cocoa.

It slips out of his hands.

Brown powder explodes, coating the air around us.

I rush to grab the bowl on the counter, my fingers grazing the edge, but my feet slip out from under me, sending me backward. My head bounces off the floor with a *crack*. Not even the pain that explodes against my skull can stop the gut-searing laugh that leaves me.

White and brown powder dust every speck of air. Slimy egg yolks drip down the counter, and then there's Silas. Kneeling next to me, his perfect prince smile is tilted to one side, splitting his face between a mix of concern and amusement. It's the thick gooey mess plastered over his cheeks and chest, and his usual slick-backed hair that's now a chaos of chocolate both in color and powder that sends me over.

No amount of effort could stop my laughs.

"Are you okay?"

"I guess your cookies are a bust." My gut tightens the harder I laugh.

"It's fine. That was the fifth batch." He stands, offering his hand. If I hadn't hit my head so hard, I would have pushed it away, but I'm not entirely sure I won't lose my balance when I stand. Reluctantly, I take it.

"Why would you make this much?" I ask.

He hauls me up, using his free hand to spot my waist with the same concern I have about falling back. Sure enough, the second I straighten out, I sway with an intense rush that has the room spinning around me. That's when I spot the corner of the kitchen layered with rows of treats: brownies, pies, and cookies, enough to host another party, all wrapped with little red bows.

It reminds me of the leftovers I package and sneak to the orphanage back home. No child should starve when the royal castles, manors, and palaces are filled with too much extra food that end up in the trash. It's simply not fair.

Before either of us gets a chance to say another word, the door slams open. Holden fills the frame, taking in the mess we made.

Why does this feel wrong? Like I'm caught in the middle of something I shouldn't be doing?

Because you're supposed to kill Silas, not laugh with him.

Holden lets out a long whistle. "What are you two doing up so early?"

Early? How long has Silas been awake?

"I was showing Silas why my specialty is not in the kitchen." Holden's lips twitch into a sly smile that matches mine. "I'm going to get cleaned up."

I'm angling to pass Holden when he grabs my arm and leans into my ear. "Meet me back here when you're done. We're going to town." He whispers too low for Silas to hear.

"You want a quick spar, brother?" Silas' voice returns to its usual hard, threatening tone. I sneak a glance back and see his jaw has tightened and his shoulders have returned to their tense stance.

I keep myself from sprinting back to my room when that's all I want to do. If Holden wants to meet with me, this could very well be my chance to widen that wedge between the brothers, to see if there's any chance of him helping me.

Before you lose your nerve.

I would never.

"Oh, Eva." Aspen stands outside my doors with her guards huddled together with worried expressions. Her blue nightgown is completely soaked. "I am so sorry. I went in to wake you to come to town with us. I even started your bath, but something happened, and it broke. My father is sending someone to fix it later."

"Oh." How does one break a bath? "Can I use yours?"

"I'm headed there now, but Holden is already ready. He won't mind if you use his." Aspen takes my hand and pulls me down the hall to the room at the end.

Holden's chambers are much simpler than Silas'. It looks staged with no personality at all. The bedding is tan rather than Silas' dark blue. The table is bare except for the two knives that protrude out of the surface, and the tapestry above the unlit fireplace is of a man with his foot on top of a deer, standing proud. It almost looks like Holden, but the lighting is too dim to make it out clearly. The only other décor is a deer head above the four-poster bed.

FATEFUL CHANCE

Fitting for a huntsman.

Aspen pulls me into the washroom, where an enormous, clawed tub is already steaming with bubbles. She places a dress on the counter that I hadn't noticed her carrying. "I take long baths, so don't rush for me. I'll meet you downstairs when I'm finished," she says her orders with a sweet smile, then runs off, leaving me alone in the cold room.

It seems the more time I spend with Aspen, the sweeter she's becoming. Still punctual and to the point, only now there's a little more gentleness in her offered smiles. Such a different girl than the one I was greeted with only yesterday.

I peel off my slip, washing my face and body with a rag as much as I can before stepping into the warm bath. I hate sitting in filth, but the feeling of a hot, nearly boiling bath has always been one of my guilty pleasures. This tub has to be the biggest I've ever laid in. Large enough for three grown men.

"I'll just be a minute!" Someone shouts from the other side of the door. My heart races. Holden isn't supposed to be back. Aspen said I'd be fine here. Maybe he won't come in.

The handle turns.

I curse myself for holding such wishful thinking.

The door pushes in before I can convince myself that I'm imagining things.

My stomach can't drop any lower when the man staring back at me smirks.

"Well, well, did you get lost on your way back to your room, or is it the other brother you wanted all along?" Silas asks, shutting the door and leaning against it, showing no plans to leave. "Or was I right last night when I asked if you wanted us both?"

I pull the bubbles in to make sure he can't see me beneath the water.

"Mine was broken, and I'm not interested in being one of your shared women."

He snorts. "Whoever told you we share is trying to get under your skin. But seeing as how you're in his tub now, yet shared my bed last night, I'm starting to think you're a little liar, evil princess."

His lips lift higher, sending crimson dripping down his chin, drawing my attention to the flush in his cheeks and tousled hair. All signs of a rough tussle.

I roll my eyes. "Only because you forced me into it. Like this marriage."

"You had a choice, and you chose correctly." He pushes off the door to grab a rag off the counter. Instead of using the sink to wet it, he makes his way to the bath and dips it in the water, using it to wipe away the cocoa, sugar, and flour from his face and shoulders. "Are you ready to tell me why you want to kill me?"

I tilt my head and feign confusion. "Who said I wanted to kill you?"

"The blade at my throat. Twice now, might I add?"

"And yet I didn't cut you, did I?"

"I think you wimped out. I think you saw my handsome face and realized you couldn't go through with it. You realized what a tragedy it would be that the world would be less because of my death."

I scoff. This man is insufferably arrogant. "Please."

"Mmmm… She begs." He tosses the rag across the room.

"I was not—" The words get stuck in my throat when he unlatches his pants. "What are you doing?"

"Bathing. I'm filthy."

"You can't come in here!"

"Why not? It's big enough for at least three of me. Stick to your side, and I'll stick to mine."

"What if someone comes in?" I glance at the door again to keep from looking at his naked body lowering into the scalding water.

"My brother is being attended to by a healer." That confirms why Silas winced when he wiped away the crimson I mistook for strawberry. "Who else would you expect to join? My father? You want all three Whitehart men to yourself?" His brow rises with a triumphant smirk.

"I don't even want the one," I retort in a low voice in case anyone is outside the door. Maybe I should call for Maison. "Use your own bath!"

"Mine is occupied."

I narrow my eyes and bite my lip to remind myself to stay calm and clear-headed before the voice in my mind can rear itself. "By who?"

His eyes lift to the ceiling, exasperated. "Some guest who stayed over snuck in and thought to entice me by being naked in my bath."

I almost snort. "You're lying."

"What's so funny?" His amusement returns. "You don't think women throw themselves at me?"

"It's just… I surprised you with a knife to your throat not a day ago. I would say you need better security."

"Who's to say I didn't want the woman in my bath?"

"The fact that you ambushed me in this one."

"And who's to say I didn't rush to this one because the other one got too dirty?" His brow lifts suggestively, and I hate the sting and fury that picks at me.

My teeth clench. "We're *engaged*."

"Are you jealous?"

"Don't make a fool of me," I snap. "You made me agree to this marriage. If you embarrass me by hooking up with other women—"

"You'll what? Kill me? Isn't that what you want to do anyway?"

I glare at the prick of a prince across from me. His leg brushes mine, and I pull my knees to my chest. "You made a fool of me once before. I won't let that happen again, *Damned Prince*."

His jaw tightens at the disgraceful nickname that has been cast on him since his mother's death giving birth to him. One of the king's harlots gave birth to Holden a few weeks later. He married her and they had Aspen soon after, but that nickname never left Silas, only now, it's in hushed whispers.

The town believes he's a jinx after he accidentally killed a maid as a boy while hunting and later passed a sickness onto a visitor who spread the sickness throughout a church, which led to half the town's deaths, including Holden and Aspen's mother. When they say the *Damned Prince* brings tragedy wherever he goes, they aren't wrong.

"The Damned Prince and the Evil Princess are quite the pair. What do they say about you again? That your father keeps you locked away so no one sees or hears the wicked ramblings of the evil spirit that resides inside of you."

I'm not evil. I'm not evil. I'm not evil.

I bite my lip hard enough to draw blood. Something he notices right away by the fall of his face.

Using my feet, I flick water at him. "Screw—" He catches my ankle, tipping me back and almost drowning me as he lifts it up to examine the bottom with that same furious look he had when I told him to cut me already.

"What the fuck is this?" His grip tightens with every attempt I make to yank away from him. He pulls me in closer with little effort, lifting my other foot that holds the same burns that are making his beautiful face distort into something even more disgustingly devastating.

"Tell me."

"Just a reminder that love is dead and romance doesn't exist. Something my father—" I bite my lip.

His head angles with questions I won't be answering. "Your father did this to you?"

My wrists begin to wail from the odd angle I'm forced into to keep myself above water. With every wiggle and frustrated grunt, he doesn't let go.

Resigning, I do the one thing I can think of that might get me out of this. I let go, letting my weight fall freely under the water.

Biggest mistake of my life.

Silas releases me, but there's no time to adjust when his arms wrap around my waist and he pulls me into his lap, hugging me tight against him. "Try that again, and I'll chain you to my bed with only sponge baths for the rest of your life."

His words are that of banter, but the look on his face tells me he's completely serious. "Now, you're going to tell me what happened while we sit here. I have all day, but I should warn you that your breasts are dangerously close to my face, and I can't keep my attention from them forever."

I let out an obnoxiously huff to let him know just how vexing he is. It's his suggestive shift beneath me that has my lips moving cold and quick. "When I was younger, Mel and I thought a couple of the boys from the nearby town were cute. Our father heard about it and thought we needed to be taught a lesson. The boys we liked weren't royal; therefore, they wouldn't serve our kingdom. Apparently, our brother made that mistake by impregnating a common girl a few years before that, so he found it fitting that we dance in slippers that had been burning over the fire. It's metaphorical for not following in his footsteps."

"Was this before or after the kidnapping?" His face remains unchanged as if the next words on my lips will solidify something in his mind.

"Both times were after. He made us waltz for hours after my brother's wedding."

"That's why you don't dance." It's not a question but an acknowledgment of my comment during finger roulette. His arms loosen.

I nod and cover what I can of myself before jumping out of the tub. He either doesn't notice I'm uncomfortable or doesn't care because he takes me in without a lick of shame. "Get a good look because you'll never see it again."

"Care to wager?" All the humiliation I felt from him forcing my vulnerability dissipates.

Giving him my back, I wrap a towel around myself. "I don't need to wager when I know I won't let you see or touch me again."

"I bet I'll get you back into my bed tonight."

"Yeah? You going to carry me there again?"

"If that's what it takes."

"Is that what it takes for women to end up in your bed? I don't doubt it." I'm fumbling to lift the dress, trying my best to avoid the mirror in front of me, when I hear water splash.

"If I win…" Drops of water fall down my neck from Silas dripping behind me. My stomach dips when he takes the dress from my hands. "You tell me why you want to kill me, who sent you… everything."

"And if I win," I spin around, forcing my eyes not to trail lower than his chest. Something else catches my eye, distracting me from where he's bumping against my stomach. Instinctively, I trace the light pink scar across his throat, cursing myself for not noticing it before. It's faint but prominent. "You tell me how you got this. And the ones on your back."

He grips my wrist, stopping me from tracing the full length of the scar. His throat bobs with his hardened tone. "Deal."

Chapter Seven

We don't walk for too long, following the narrow trail through the daunting white forest, listening to the rising whispers of the wind, twigs, and snow crunching beneath our feet. The trek toward town is miserable. My feet are soaked, and I'm not entirely sure my toes haven't snapped off.

My kingdom is a few days' ride away, but I still find myself searching for the familiar spires and turrets tucked far away from the town and for the palace our false doubles live in. My father prefers privacy and would never live this close to anyone let alone a town. When I sneak out in the dead of night to leave food for the orphanage, I'm in the carriage for hours.

I wonder if Mel is there now or if she's off in another kingdom, schmoozing the princes and princesses by herself. Without me reeling her back in, Mel is either getting into more trouble than usual or being a complete wallflower without her usual audience to both annoy and entertain.

"Why did you agree to marry our brother?" Aspen's voice is light and curious. Dressed in a plain scarlet dress that's more comparable to rags than her royal dresses, her fair skin glows against the snowy backdrop. Her red lips and onyx hair accentuate her round cheeks. She looks like a girl playing with her mother's makeup.

My own dress is a simple mauve that I don't hate one bit. It's the thin peddler's cloak Aspen gave me that isn't helping with the growing chill or falling snow.

"He insisted," I answer honestly, rubbing the back of my aching neck. My head is what hit the ground so I'm not sure why my neck is so stiff.

Holden grunts beside me. "You don't take me for a girl who marries so carelessly."

"What is careless about marrying him?" I ask, noticing the split in his lip and the darkening around his eye, and I don't miss the way he favors his right leg and grabs for his ribs every couple of steps.

"He's the Damned Prince," Aspen explains as if that is answer enough. "Everything he does leads to someone else's misery."

That sounds more like my sister.

"We're all placing bets on who is going to die with the announcement of your engagement." Holden snickers, grabbing at his ribs again. "If it's any consolation, we hope it's not you."

"I can take care of myself." I stand a bit taller. The creaking and shadows in the manor are scarier than Silas with his whisk and perfect damn smile. "Maybe it's not me you should be worried about," I mutter under my breath.

Holden's grin holds a wryness I desperately want to decipher. "Maybe not."

Aspen skips a little as the town grows closer ahead of us.

"Do you need me?" Holden asks when she starts walking in another direction with her bag of books held tightly against her.

"Of course not. They're the usual clients, so no need for your muscle today, Huntsman." She winks and runs off.

"What is she doing?"

He looks down at me like he doesn't want to answer, like he's worried and would rather follow her. "Handing out books." He tells me they're romances, but when I tell him that's my favorite, he responds coldly, "Not that kind."

My curiosity piques, but I don't press him. I don't have the words to. All the questions that form flutter away at the sight of the vanishing black shadow at the end of the alley. Like a passing apparition, the glimpse of that familiar white face has my heart beating a little faster, has me second-guessing my sanity once again.

With Maison and the other guards searching for the missing Digby, Holden's presence is the only thing keeping me from running ahead to search for him.

He's not here, I remind myself. *He doesn't exist.* I take a deep breath and rub my temple, erasing the Phantom from my mind. *You make this up when you're in public. He's not real. You're safe. You don't need him.*

I was going to stay behind, but after my run-in with Silas, I figured the fresh air wouldn't be the worst idea. I need to get my head on straight and recollect myself, or I'll go stir-crazy over the next few weeks. My delirium has only worsened since being here.

The town itself isn't too busy. There aren't many people walking about, but then again, the sun is hidden by the gray billowing clouds and white blanket of fog rolling in. As we get farther along, I understand the need for our simple attire. No one gives us a second glance as we make our way down the alleys, passing a bakery that smells of fresh bread and lemon, a blacksmith with a plethora of daggers, swords, and arrows that I admire but don't need, an apothecary Mel would love, and a dress shop that displays simple dresses similar to the one I have on.

It's the black one in the back that catches my eye, but we're moving too fast for me to fully admire it.

"You want to go in?" Holden takes a few steps back. I almost laugh at the idea of this massive man surrounded by pretty fabrics and jewels.

"They're closed."

He limps back to the shop and raps on the door with a firm, unintentional force, like a man who doesn't know his own strength. A slender man at least a decade older than us, points to the closed sign, unlatching the locks immediately when he sees Holden holding up a bag of coins to the window. "The lady wants to see the dark stuff."

We step into the cozy shop surrounded by a variety of fabrics, differing in color, style, cut, and material. From the outside, the clothing appeared simple, but upon closer observation, I find dresses with the detail I admire: the embroidered stitching and laced edging. "Are you… You're not Grim Rose, are you?"

"I am not, but I carry her dresses. She's a friend." The man looks impressed that I would know such a name. His delicate fingers run down one of the dresses with true admiration. "You have a good eye."

"My sister-in-law introduced me to her work. Are you friends with her? Directly? Does she come here? I can't tell you how big of an admirer I am. Her lace detail and the off-color stitching, and the—"

"Sheer skirt layers that accentuate the built-in corset."

"Exactly!" I agree, taking in the way we describe the rich indigo dress that I can't bear to look away from. It's breathtaking. "It's beauty and rebellion built in an elegant dress."

The man leans in and whispers softly. "Poison or weapons?"

I giggle. One cannot be a true admirer of Grim Rose without understanding that question.

Lowering my voice to his soft tone, I answer, "Daggers."

Holden surveys us both cluelessly. The sight of him is exactly how I imagined—all muscle surrounded by lace and silk. A hunter who should be covered in blood, looking somehow perturbed yet not entirely uninterested in the elegant, sultry surroundings.

I can't say I'm not affected by the stark contrast.

"This one is perfect for you, then." I could hug the shop owner for ripping me away from the Holden-sized distraction. He's the only man I've met who knows about Grim Rose—women's best-kept secret. Her designs feature hidden pockets that conceal weapons to help women stave off attackers.

"How many Grim Roses do you have?"

"Seven, plus this one makes eight."

"I'll take them all." I pull out my coin bag, ready to give him everything I have.

Holden stops me before I can untie it. "Allow me."

"I cannot. I just ordered eight dresses. You can't possibly—"

"The one condition is you wear that one right now." A coil of heat knots low in my belly at the demanded request, unsure if I like it or—

We like it.

Do you want spiders or feathers today? A memory of that harsh, distorted voice assaults my mind. The choices he would give me were part of the mental torture, and the reason I now despise being given choices. Did it matter if I picked spiders? No, it only meant he started with them.

My eyes tighten, but it's a mistake that puts me back in a darkness I've longed to forget, the one with a bag over my head and light crawling tickling my skin. When I open them, Holden's giving me a look I can't decipher from worry, confusion, or curiosity.

"Sorry." I clear my throat. "Headache." I rub my temples.

The shop owner holds the indigo dress up to my body. "You, Princess Evangeline, are going to look immaculate in this."

"Wait," I grab the man's arm before he can turn away, "how do you know who I am?"

His pink cheeks turn a hue darker. "I— Please, forgive me, princess. I used to be your kingdom's personal tailor long ago. You were much younger. I wouldn't expect you to remember. I was removed while you were… *away*."

"Removed? Why?" My childhood is a blur, especially during that time, but surely I would remember someone as passionate as him.

"Your father removed everyone in your kingdom's service at the time. It was a safety precaution due to what happened to you. He hired all new staff with a much harder protocol for employment. Those of us who did reapply were never readmitted, not even after your return."

FATEFUL CHANCE

A bitter weight sinks in my chest. "I'm so sorry." I stayed in my room for over a year after I came back. I didn't see anyone except Mel, Cain, and eventually Maison, who was a new guard.

His hand covers mine, the bandage around his fingers scratching against mine. "Please, never apologize. What happened to you was awful. And you were so young. I don't think any of us could be angry with you if we wanted to." He pulls back with a sincere expression that has shame and regret eating me from the inside. "Give me a minute? I'll bag everything up and then help you into that one. I have treats on the counter while you wait."

"What happened when you were younger?" Holden asks once the man is out of sight.

I shake my head, my fingers flipping the red ruby around my neck. Holden tracks the movement like the hunter he is. "It was long ago. I rather not relive it."

"Sometimes it helps."

"Sometimes it doesn't." I snap with more venom than I intended. It's been a decade, but the bitter rage inside of me is more potent than ever, especially now that I'm so close to ridding myself of the man who summoned it.

Before either of us can say another word that could bring forth even worse memories, I grab the dress and head for the dressing room on my own.

Noticing the mirror on the far wall, I turn to keep it at my back, cursing myself once I'm alone.

He was only asking a fair question.

He's nosy.

It's the mistake I made that cost so many people their jobs that has me turning against myself. I just wanted to know where Mel snuck off to at night. I wasn't ten feet into the woods before a bag was shoved over my head. I woke sometime later with my hands bound behind my back by ropes that sliced into my skin the more I struggled.

Following Mel had been the biggest mistake of my life. It cost me not only my sanity but the livelihood of all those who served our family at that time.

I should have known there would be consequences for disobedience. I've known punishment all my life but never realized it could be inflicted on those around me.

With the sudden need to leave, I remove my old dress to change as quickly as I can.

How can I ever repay all those people?

Stepping in, I slip the new dress up and over my hips, bringing it flush around my torso. It's impossible not to admire the way the bones in the corset sit perfectly along my ribs and lift my breasts a little higher. I'm not usually the twin who likes to show off my assets, but it would be a shame not to in a dress like this.

The final touch is the small dagger engraved with Silas' initial that slides perfectly up the corset's center.

"Do you need help?" Holden calls from outside the curtain.

Yes!

No.

FATEFUL CHANCE

Grim Rose dresses tie specifically so the wearer doesn't need any assistance. "Do you know how to tie a corset?" I call out, rhetorically.

The satin curtain flies open and Holden steps in, filling the already tight space. I'm forced back against the mirror at an odd angle that twists me around while he moves to close the partition.

When I lift my head, a wave of nausea rips straight through me.

My face, the real one, stares back at me. My dark eyeshadow, my mascara, and my powdered cheeks—*my mask*—is gone, leaving me bare in more ways than one. My gaze drops to my feet.

I washed my face before Silas interrupted me in the bath and threw off my entire routine. I never reapplied my mask. Not even my hair is tied in its usual braided bun atop my head. No wonder my neck aches. The bun pulls my chin higher, and I've been walking with my head facing my feet all the way to town.

I let my guard down.

Without speaking, Holden pulls the strings behind my back and begins tying them in the proper corset style. It has the option to tie in the front, but I don't stop him. Tempering my rapid heartbeat and avoiding my own reflection is difficult enough.

"Do you help a lot of women put their clothes back on?" I tease.

"I'm better at taking them off." His lips tilt, doing no favors at steadying my pulse. I can feel the rush of heat rising to my cheeks. "I assure you, hog-tying an unwilling body is far more difficult than lacing a corset." He pulls at the lace, taking my breath with it, tightening and loosening where he needs to, up and down my back. It's soothing, being taken care of. Different than when Aspen tugged and yanked at me.

My eyes close, letting him work.

When he stops, they fly open, meeting his dark ambers in the mirror.

"Why did you stop?"

"You… never mind." His throat visibly bobs as he goes back to tying my back.

"I, what?"

He clears his throat, his fingers working the laces faster. "You moaned."

"I did not!" I would have heard if I did. Wouldn't I? How are these men taking my guard down so easily?

Our eyes stay locked on each other. His hand slowly slides from my back to the side of my ribs, where it was a second ago, only I'm aware of it now. Using his other hand, he pulls a lace, bringing my back against his hard chest. Sure enough, a moan rolls out of me.

"Holden!" I yell in a hushed tone. "I didn't mean to—"

"Don't apologize, little doe." He lets out a grumbled laugh, finishing the final tie. I fully expected him to leave without turning back, to find Silas when we return so they can make fun of how entrapped I get in their presence.

But again, he takes me by surprise. His fingers slither and tighten just under my breast, his other hand falls to the top of my hip as he leans into the crook of my neck. "There isn't a sweeter sound I'd rather hear."

I don't know if I'm mortified or titillated.

FATEFUL CHANCE

Titillated!

Mortified!

I can never agree with the voices. We're at constant odds. She either wants me to feel horrible or aroused when I want to feel confident or normal.

A brief glance reflects bright pink cheeks in the girl I refuse to acknowledge. I don't need to look to remember what I just saw. The way my dark brows naturally arch, how my bottom lip is plumper than the top. I'm the spitting image of Mel, only with green eyes, black hair, and... gentler.

When did I get so gentle? It has to be the lack of makeup.

Or the lack of killing.

_We've_—I've _literally never killed anyone. Calm down._

I look weak, like the coward my father promises I am. A _pretty_ coward because I could never disrespect Mel by calling myself otherwise, but still an ambivalent girl who will never be normal.

"Have you ever hunted?" Holden interrupts my self-hatred.

The change in topic takes me a second to adjust, but I am thankful for it. Anything to get me away from my own reflection, figuratively and literally. "Once. I killed a pig and felt so awful, I threw up and didn't eat meat for a month."

"A pig?" He doesn't hide how unimpressed he is. "They basically stand there and let you kill them."

"It was really far away." My voice heightens as I defend my one kill. It made me sick, in private, of course, but it made my father proud that I wasn't too weak to kill it. It had been my first lesson in becoming *cold and calculating.*

"Princess?" The store owner calls.

"I'm here!" I jump out of the curtain partition, instantly aware of Holden's lack of touch. The man claps his cheeks with his hands. "Oh my, Eva… I'm sorry, Princess Evangeline. You look mesmerizing. It could not have found a better body to grace. Truly."

"Please." I wave my hand, my stomach knotting at the memory of Silas in the bath earlier, *"She begs."*

"You're too kind, I promise," I add, feeling suddenly shy.

"He's not." Holden comes out of the curtains. "It's breathtaking."

I bite my lip to keep from smiling too hard. I'm not one to be on the receiving end of compliments.

"All your dresses are here." The shop owner points to the boxes. "But I did want to gift you one final thing." The man ushers me back behind the curtain, shutting us from Holden's view. He wraps his arms around my shoulders and shows me the black choker with a white standing, flared collar. "This is one of Grim Rose's new accessories reserved for those with special tastes. The choker bit here has two slits that can hide tiny weapons, those of an ingested sort." He winks. "And your necklace will pair perfectly on top of it. Do you mind?"

I nod and close my eyes.

Unclasping the shackle around my neck, he places the new collar on, quickly layering the ruby necklace back on top. I'm more than grateful he doesn't say anything about the prominent scar.

I want nothing more than to hide from the mirror, maybe smash it into a few hundred pieces, but with the man so elated behind me, it would be rude not to take in the ensemble he's visibly eager and waiting for me to acknowledge. A quick glance tells me all I need to know: Grim Rose is the perfect name for whoever created such an immaculate design because that's exactly what I look like.

"You are stunning, princess. This piece is on me." He grips my shoulders with a snug embrace and reopens the curtains.

"Wow." Holden's head bobs, holding all seven boxes. "It's... extra."

"Extra beautiful," the man corrects him with a low snarl. "Oh, you didn't want any treats? I swear, when we're blessed with these..." His eyes roll to the sky with a hum of pleasure. "You have to take some." He stacks the familiar treat wrapped with the red bow on top of the other boxes in Holden's arms. "He's a strong boy, I'm sure he can manage a few brownies and cookies. Oh, and there's this creamy strawberry pie you'll die for."

The man gives me another dreamy face as I grab one, unravel the bow, and take a bite. Sure enough, the brownie holds the same mouthwatering, melting texture Silas' had.

"To die for," I agree, placing my entire coin bag on the counter. I don't know or care if Holden paid him already. This man deserves every bit after I cost him his livelihood. "Thank you for everything, and please tell Grim Rose I am her biggest admirer."

"Of course, Princess." He lowers to a curt bow.

"I'm sorry, I didn't catch your name."

"Strix." He takes my offered hand and shakes it with more enthusiasm after I tell him to simply call me Eva.

We say our goodbyes and Holden leads us out of the store, down the cobblestone path once again. The chilly wind has picked up tenfold, sending an icy shiver straight through us.

The brute next to me doesn't complain about holding the boxes or give in when I offer to lighten his load by at least one. Instead, he asks, "Do you drink?"

A laugh belts out of me before I can hide it. "I pref-ffer food." With my stutter and chattering teeth, I realize I left the thin cloak back at the shop. It didn't do much, but even I can admit that bare arms in the middle of a snowstorm isn't the wisest decision.

"My favorite tavern is up on this corner. They have the best ale around. Even if you don't drink, they'll have something you'll enjoy."

The thought of drinking sends my head into a spiraling mess, but I try my best to hide it with a smile rather than explaining to him that I detest the taste, being out of control, and the way it causes the voices in my head to grow louder and hallucinations to become more vivid.

Luckily, I know how to fake my drinks. A couple of spills here and there or tossing it into a nearby plant usually does the trick. I've even taken my glass to the washroom to refill half of it with water.

As we near the tavern, I notice a peddler pushing jewelry and flowers, a desperate attempt at survival in the winter. I tell Holden to go ahead without me while I look at what she has.

I wait until the Tavern door closes to approach the hunchback woman. "What are you still doing here, Dove?"

FATEFUL CHANCE

Her young eyes meet mine while the rest of her appears to be a decrepit older woman on her deathbed. Gripping the back of my neck, she forces me toward her, her head swiveling back and forth before whispering so low I wouldn't be able to hear her if my ear weren't against her lips. "Leave it, Eva. I'm not here for you. This is personal." The plea in her voice is one I feel to my core. "*Please*, don't tell your brother or Duke."

In a hurry to be rid of me, she hands me a handful of carnations, her sights locking on something behind me.

When I turn, my eyes remain wide and focused so as not to lose him. I ask her if she sees him, too, shrouded in black: pants, shirt, cloak, hood, with his white mask barely visible in the falling snow.

"I see him all the time."

My mouth opens with questions, needing an explanation, when someone squeezes my shoulders. "Come on, little doe." Holden pulls me away. "We have to get inside. There's a storm coming."

Chapter Eight

It's barely morning, and the tavern is busy and bustling. The town isn't dead after all, they're all here, drinking the day away. From the sounds of it, this is their tradition during a winter storm, huddling in the local tavern, getting completely blitzed until it passes.

Mugs and glasses of ale, whisky, and bubbling wine are all among the variety of drinks layering the sticky tables and clinking together while someone belts a raunchy bar ballad from the corner.

I spot my dress boxes safely tucked behind the bar, where I follow Holden to the stools. More of Silas' wrapped treats scatter along the counter, and I wonder if he makes them for the entire town often.

He's so sweet.

He's horrid.

This doesn't seem like something our captor would do.

No, I agree. My captor only gave me a bite of a sour apple once a week to keep me from keeling over.

"Two lagers, two shots of whisky, and two champagnes."

"Who in all the thrones are you ordering that for?" I openly gawk at him like the maniac he is if he thinks I'm touching one of those.

"Us."

"I *cannot* drink all of that."

"I bet you can drink all of this and one more beer." He smiles, and again, I'm reminded of Silas and our bet. I will most definitely not be ending up in his bed tonight. If I drink all of this, I won't be leaving this tavern alive.

"And if I can't?"

"That's not how that works. If you drink all of this," he leans into my ear, his temple brushing mine. "I'll help you do exactly what you set out to do here, *little Reaper.*"

I pull away, panic tightening my chest. "You?"

Holden grabs a lock of my hair and pulls me back into him. "And if you don't finish all the drinks, let's say you stay in my room tonight, where you can convince me to help you anyway. Only misery and tragedy follow my brother, after all. The world will be a better place without him."

My mouth dries at every promise made over the last minute, the name he calls me in those diaries, the figment of my imagination... he's real and sitting right next to me.

I can't think straight. Ten years. It's been ten years of him hiding in the shadows, behind that mask, only to come out publicly in a crowded tavern. Why not any of the times he had me at his fingertips? Why hide at all?

The barkeep places all six drinks in front of us. Holden grabs the flute first and holds it up with a questioning smirk.

I lift the whisky in the air. "*When* I finish all of these, you'll tell me everything, starting with why you'd help me and why you've been watching me."

With the clink of our glasses, his lips lift even higher in silent agreement. I don't wait to toss back the warm amber liquid, too scared I'll lose my nerve if I don't act quickly.

My eyes water at the familiar thick spice, and it's not just because of the taste. The burn singes my throat—once my dry mouth's only reprieve.

The voice in my head screams for me to stop.

"Next."

"Easy, doe." Holden pats my shoulder and the scent of metal, leather, and pepper overcomes me. "We'll be here all day with that storm. Pace yourself."

I hold the flute high. The sooner this is over with, the sooner I can stop drinking and wait for my own storm to pass. The voice is going to be unmanageable in about ten minutes.

I don't wait for him to clink my glass this time. I take down half of the champagne until the bubbles are too much, and I'm forced to stop.

"If you're worried about me knowing your secret, I promise I won't tell anyone." His palm lands on my knee in what I assume is supposed to be comforting but only makes me more aware of his ability to overpower me, more so after this alcohol takes full effect. He wouldn't have to order my death if he wanted to do it himself with a quick squeeze of his hand around my neck.

FATEFUL CHANCE

He had that hand around my neck last night, proving just how easy it is for him to kill me, how easy it is for him to coax me into letting him.

He's Silas' brother, surely, he wouldn't really wish him dead.

With every passing second, I feel the noose tightening around my throat. I'm missing something. Forcing Maison to stay behind might have been a mistake. He would be able to pick up on what I'm not able to.

Holden's massive form gave me a familiar comfort and sense of safety I found in Maison, but knowing he's my Phantom, that he might be willing to murder his brother, I'm realizing this man is more complex than he presents.

"I brought you here to have a good time. You can slow down and enjoy yourself."

Taking in the breath he's begging me to take, I relent and swivel on the stool to observe the rest of the bar. Part of me envies how easy it is for these people to let themselves be so carefree and vulnerable in front of one another, but mostly, I judge them for how weak they expose themselves. If someone came in here to attack the place, most of them wouldn't know until it's too late.

"The only time I've ever been drunk was by force, and I promise you it wasn't enjoyable." It's another normal thing I can't experience like the rest of them: dancing, dating, or simply eating.

Envy slithers her way back up. They say she's a green monster and that eyes are the windows to the soul. Maybe that's why mine are so vibrantly that color. Born a princess, haunted by delusions, driven by vengeance, yet aching and desperate for a normal life I'll never have.

"I'm The Huntsman. No one's going to hurt you while I'm here, and I'm not leaving you, so again, *enjoy* yourself. And stop looking at me like I'm going to kill you. I only wanted you to know I knew your secret so you have someone you can trust."

"I trust no one, and I don't need you to protect me." My giggles echo into the flute at the thought of feeling protected by the Phantom I thought I created in my mind for years over the massive man next to me with his promises.

Finishing the flute, I reach for the lager next.

With his hand on my knee, he spins me back to the bar, his face a breath away from mine. His dark glare holds a plea of impatience. "What will it take for you to trust me?"

I lean in closer, brushing my lips past his as I tuck a loose strand behind his ear and whisper, "Only those unworthy of trust ask that ridiculous question."

Movement in the corner catches my attention and a sinking feeling settles in the pit of my stomach.

Keeping my sights on that spot, I finish the lager, stopping only twice for air. "I need to use the washroom." I stumble off the stool, feeling Holden's watching gaze follow me toward the back hallway.

Once out of his view, I grab the wall to steady myself. The last thing I need is Holden knowing just how much of a lightweight I am. At this point, I'm not sure if it's in my head or if the floor is actually tilting. The building is older, it's entirely possible the floorboards shift with the right amount of pressure.

Pushing in the first door I see, I find a full kitchen with a man in an apron cooking away. The next door leads to the men's washroom, where a few men look back, offering suggestive whistles and winks.

I follow the hallway to the left and stop.

That princely smile is unmistakable, even with his brown hair no longer slicked back but free to curl wildly. His royal attire is replaced with the same dark cloak Holden wore.

He doesn't see me.

Why would he, with a woman like that in front of him?

Shut up!

The woman he's leading through a door drops her robe, revealing a dress that leaves her petite back exposed. I would have considered her a typical woman with a horrible taste in men if I hadn't spotted the wedding band on the wrong hand, grabbing my *fiancé's* collar just before the door shut.

Harlot. One of the widowed whores who are whispered about. My sister-in-law used to be one, so I'm finding it harder not to hate the woman. They're supposed to be less obvious, but apparently, this one doesn't care about being discreet and with a prince, no less. An *engaged* prince. Didn't I tell him not to make a fool of me?

I push in the last door, finding myself in the women's washroom. Latching the stall shut, I sit on the toilet to steady myself.

My head is spinning. I should go in there, confront them, make a scene. That's what Mel would do. But then what? He'll always be able to find another harlot to fuck. His days are numbered anyway, so he might as well have his fun.

My bottom lip puffs out in the most pitiful frown. I don't know why I'm disappointed. I found my Phantom, and he's willing to help me complete my task and rid myself of Silas once and for all. I still have to wait until after the wedding to secure Tydas' alliance, but my plan is coming along little by little.

Smack! I slap myself. *Get it together!*

Killing him isn't going to get rid of you, is it? I ask the voice.

No. I'll be keeping you company until we're withering in the cold, dark ground, little lunatic.

The bathroom door bursts open.

Great, my time alone to aggressively catch my breath and talk to myself is over. I slap myself again to shake out the voice. The laugh comes involuntarily.

I steady myself one last time before unlatching the bathroom stall. One step, and I'm stumbling forward, landing headfirst into something hard.

"Bleeding fucking thrones!" I curse myself, pushing off whatever I just hit.

It definitely isn't a wall.

Someone grabs my waist and pushes me against the stall post. "That mouth on you is cute," the dark voice purrs. "But you don't use it to drink."

The white-faced man.

My phantom.

"Holden, why are you wearing that?" My words slur. I graze the cold white mask with my fingertips, laughing as I tap on it. "Let me see thy face."

"How much have you had?" He sounds angry, but it's hard to tell with the frozen white face set in place. It's scarier up close, and with the daylight trickling in through the window, casting a light gleam over the unmoving expression, my insides quiver. For once, I can see it perfectly: the oversized, pointy square smile etched into it, the eye holes that are too small to make out the color behind them.

I hold my fingers up to count. "A whisky, a chaaampagne, a laaager."

"Trying to outdrink Holden? That's not a good plan."

"We made a deal and I won." I beam up at the very real, very haunting Phantom. "Now yooou have to tell meee why you've been following me forever." I wait for an explanation that never comes, frowning harder. "Holden—"

"I'm not Holden."

"But," my brows hurt from frowning so hard, "he called me little Reaper."

His head tilts, giving me chills that have nothing to do with the winter storm brewing outside. "And where do I call you that?"

My diary.

Fury prickles at my chest. "That fucking bastard!"

His fingers slip to the new collar around my neck. Taking a step back, he trails his other hand down the sides of the new corset, taking the sheer skirt between his fingers. "Every time I think you couldn't be more perfect, you find a way to make that word unworthy of you."

My spine tightens. My pulse stutters, beating faster, thudding against the necklace. Hearing his written words in his deep voice transcends me to a place only he can. Every sight of him has always sent a shameful shudder through me, every written word has filled me with flutters, and his voice… his voice terrifies me, making me feel things I shouldn't, thinking the impossible.

"I have to go." He takes my hand into his, the other sweeping up my neck, shifting so nothing but my corset and his tunic separates us. "Swear you won't drink any more tonight. I don't need you out of your right mind."

My inner voice laughs. **He doesn't know you at all to think you have one of those.**

I giggle, nodding my answer with a smile that refuses to fall. Without another word, he leaves, taking what little sanity I have left with him.

With him gone, that sinking feeling in the pit of my stomach stirs, turning into a flurry of boiling rage I don't often feel.

He doesn't get to watch me for years, give me cathartic slivers of happiness with his notes and fingers—**don't forget tongue**—tongue, and order me around with his seductive voice, and then leave. All on *his* terms. Absolutely not.

Storming out of the washroom, I rush down the hallways, finding his black cloak disappearing through the kitchen door. I stumble toward it, throwing the door open.

Everyone in the kitchen turns, but I pay them no mind when I find the person I'm looking for making a quick line toward the back. The side of his white mask gives me all the motivation I need to remain steady on my feet as I zigzag my way through the cooks and push the back door wide open.

FATEFUL CHANCE

A sheet of icy air slices at my skin. Snow isn't just falling, it's swirling in uncontrollable winds that send my hair blowing over my face and toward the sky.

The rolling fog is too thick to see clearly, but I spot his black figure in the distance. Keeping my arms around my chest, I follow him.

Phantom

This little Reaper is quite literally going to be the death of me.

I thought I was imagining her voice but when I turn around, there she is, shivering with skin so pale, it's iridescent. I shouldn't find her this beautiful while she's slowly dying of hyperthermia, but the way she's desperately calling out for me has me dazed, entrapped by that black magic she naturally possesses.

I follow her voice, finding her stumbling through the thickening snow in nothing but that stunning dress that threatens any sense of control I have. She's soaking wet from the harsh blizzard, and with how much alcohol she drank, she probably doesn't even realize how cold she is.

I'm so pissed off that I don't say anything as I scoop her into my arms, holding her as close to me as physically possible, and rush toward the cabin. In a matter of ten minutes, I'm pushing through the door and laying her in front of the fireplace I left ablaze. As quickly as I can, I start removing every wet layer.

Her small hands tremble on mine to stop me. "I have to take them off, or you'll die." I don't make the argument that I've seen her naked more times than I can count, or that I've felt her body shudder this same way without the cold threatening her life.

She moves to help, but I'm faster. I don't bother with the laces, and instead, pull the blade from behind my back to cut them away until I'm able to pull the dress clean off her.

Her undergarments aren't too wet, but I slip them off too, followed by her bracelets, necklace, and the flared collar that makes her look regal.

I falter when I see the deep scars around her wrist and take in the brutal one along her neck. She's been through hell, but it feels like I'm in it. My blood boils thinking of the torture she went through to get these.

Grabbing the furs, duvet, and sheets from the bed, I tuck them around her. I bring the water and bread I had waiting for me on the nightstand, kick off my clothes, and settle in behind her. Wrapping her in my arms, I pull her flush against me. She sucks in a tight breath but doesn't argue.

With her so out of it, I toss the mask and wait for her body to stop shivering. "Why did you follow me?"

Her teeth chatter louder than the crackling of the fire, but I need her awake. "I—I n-neded to know you're r-reeal. That you're not a h-h-haaallucination." She pauses, and I wait for her inner arguments to play out through her trembling jaw. "C-caaan't you feel him? Heee's definitely not a hallucination." Another pause. "Nooo, he's not. The a-aasshole cut my dress."

A gut-pinching laugh escapes me before I can think to mask it. "That's not how I intended to get you out of your dress."

Her neck starts to twist back. I hurry to position the mask back in place. "Why have *yooou* been following *meee?*"

I'm too aware of her small body against mine, how ice-cold her skin is, how soft she is. There's no barrier between us to hide how she's affecting me, and by the sharp whisky-scented inhale she takes, she feels me pressed against her thighs.

I've always kept her at a distance, but seeing her unsteady eyes search for mine, I remind myself that only one thing will ever keep us apart again; her word, *coffin*. One day, the mask will come off, and she'll use it, but by whatever fateful chance that brought us together, however short it may be, I'm not wasting any time I get with her. Any time she's willing to give me.

She repeats her question, and I don't have it in me to lie or deny her an answer this time. "The way revenge has been your one and only obsession, you've been mine."

She shifts, twisting all the way around to face me. Her hand drapes over my chest under the thick layers of blankets. "Why?" she asks, her inner augments following rapidly. "He's obviously crazy." Pause. "He's not crazy, we're—*I'm* crazy."

I tighten my arms around her shoulders and lift the mask over my chin, enough to place my lips on her forehead. "You're not crazy, beautiful."

The gentle hum that leaves her brings both of our awareness to how vehemently she's affecting me all over again, only now I'm pressed against the bottom of her stomach. "Body heat," I say as an explanation for why we're in this position and completely naked.

The silence wraps a blanket of tranquility around us with the sound of the crackling fire, the feel of its heat on our faces, our limbs tangled. Our legs slowly snake in and out of one another, her palm exploring every muscle like she's counting how many I have—across my chest, down my arm, around my torso until she stalls at the prominent V.

I don't hesitate to sweep my touch over her, though I'm not as gentle as she is. Soft touches take her to a place that makes her hands fist and eyes tighten, but the needy grasps and carnal clawing melt her entire body into mine.

When my thumb slides across her nipple, her forehead lands on my chest with a moan that has me twirling it between my fingers, tugging lightly, and increasing the pressure until I get the sultry reaction I'm looking for.

She touches the side of my mask as her leg hooks my hip. Her lips trail moaning kisses across my upper body. "Light blue book." *Kiss.* "Page 23."

A determination lights behind her viridian eyes, dragging me in deeper.

Her hand leaves my mask to wrap around where I'm hard between us. The cold touch steals a sharp breath from me.

My gut hollows out, knowing the exact book and scene she's referencing.

"For warmth." Her voice is low and tender as her palm slides up and down my shaft.

I should stop her, she's drunk, but the weaker side of me wins out because I can't take my eyes off her. Not when her head tucks against my chest and she watches herself work me.

She's going to chalk this up to a dream by tomorrow unless I leave hers with something that she can't deny is real, but other than putting a baby inside of her, she'll only convince herself that any mark on her was created by herself.

That thought of marking her brings me closer to the edge. The fire has nothing to do with how hot my skin burns as her pace quickens, using drops that seep out of my tip to help her.

If she weren't drunk, I'd take her right here, but that's a moment I want her to remember, and not as the man she thinks isn't real.

I'm on the verge of cumming when she stops. Her head vanishes under the covers, positioning herself between my legs. She's not slow, but I'm aware of every damn second it takes for her to get there.

I've never been more weak. Lifting to my elbows, I toss the covers off her head and lean back to watch her lips wrap around me. Her wet tongue drags over and around my crown.

Holding me steady in her palm, she licks up and down the part of me that's been begging for her, recreating the scene in that book to every last letter. I know she's never done this before, but she looks like she knows exactly what she's doing, or at least enjoying it.

Most women put on an over-the-top show or deep throat to be done with it, but not Eva. Eva looks at my dick like it's her favorite fucking toy. "You really like this, don't you?"

Her eyes find mine like she forgot I was here.

As she works to put me further in her mouth, her free hand rests her on my thigh, her head bobbing a little farther back every time. "That's it, little Reaper. Take me slow." The greens in her eyes nearly vanish every time I speak, and as much as I live to see that vibrant color in them, I love the way I'm affecting her even more. The way all of my words affect her, written or spoken.

When her head remains in place a little longer, I realize what she's doing. I run my hands through her sable waves, my groans encouraging her.

"Tell me," Her cheeks redden, and her throat flutters in protest. She moves to retreat but I hold her, keeping her in place. "Do figments of your imagination make you choke like I do, little Reaper?"

Her throaty moan vibrates the base of my spine, and fuck, if I didn't have control... My hips tense, naturally wanting to jerk further into her, but I don't. A quick release only means she's done, and I'm not done with her. "Don't be afraid. I'll bring you back. I always do."

Her round eyes fill with tears, her grip on my thighs loosening. I let her go. "Good girl. Breathe for me." Her head jerks back, keeping me at the tip of her tongue as she sucks down air.

Before I order *again*, I'm back in her mouth. A deep groan leaves my throat as she works her tongue around me, using me to cut off her breath to take herself to that in-between place so I can save her.

I'm right there with her when she lowers her hand between her legs. "Mm. Your breath is mine, isn't it?" My fingers tighten in her hair as she moans against me, her eyes flickering to mine. "Your pleasure, your life, your pretty little mind. All mine." This time, when water fills her lash line, I buck my hips.

Her throat flutters as her head naturally jerks back, but she digs her fingers into my thighs, pulling herself right back in place. "Look at you, Eva. Taking everything I give you and begging for more."

The sight of her trying to get herself off while pleasuring me is an erotic sight that I can't edge myself from any further. I let her go, watching her back rise and fall as she catches her breath, using her hand to work me.

My lungs fill with hers. There isn't a place, here, there, or the in-between where she can go that I won't feel her, that I won't find her and pull her to my side.

She's exhausted. From the air taken from her, the drinks, the cold… It's been too much in such a short amount of time. But as her eyes grow heavy, the green in them returns with even more vibrancy and determination. "You're going to take all of me, aren't you, little Reaper?"

The moment her tongue circles under my tip, I'm done for. I fist her hair. My entire body tenses beneath her as I find my release. I fully expect to see me spill out of her mouth, but she's swallowing as I'm cumming, and that realization only draws me out longer.

I lie back and pinch the ridge of my nose, forgetting I have the stupid mask on, trying to catch my unsteady breath.

I have no words, *no words*, as she crawls on top of me, settling her legs perfectly under my shoulders. She steadies herself using the fireplace mantle and reaches down to pull my mask enough to expose what she needs, lowering herself onto my tongue.

"I don't mind being crazy if I get to see you." She lets out a heated whimper as I suck her clit into my mouth, throbbing all over again at her taking what she wants without question. "You're the only part of my life that makes me feel normal when I'm anything but."

Her admission has me cupping her ass, keeping her against my face while I roll us over, careful to lay her back on the covers.

While I appreciate her riding my face like she didn't just swallow my dick like a hardworking harlot, I want her comfortable while I'm worshipping her.

"So, yes," she pants. "All of me is yours. I've been yours for years."

"Is that my fucking sister?!" Cain steps into the cabin, his fists at his sides, stalking toward Eva, asleep on my bed. She looks too tiny and fragile in it.

If there was another place to take her, I would have, but the storm is still strong, and this is where I meet the Trove every month. Looking them over now, there's no need for my personal services.

Duke, silent as always, takes one step inside and leans against the wall. He's known to infiltrate himself into any situation and group brilliantly, but I've only ever seen this side of him. The silent observer.

"Keep your voice down and masks ready if she wakes," I reprimand Cain, also known as Death, and pull him back to the front table before he can think to wake her. "Holden got her drunk, and she followed me here. I don't need her knowing who I am yet."

"She doesn't even—" Cain's fist finds my chin too quickly to stop the blow completely, but I dodge enough of the force for it not to leave a mark. "You're fucking my sister, and she doesn't even know who you are?"

Duke snickers. "Look who's stalking—I mean talking."

"That's not the same!" Cain yells at him over his shoulder. His head falls back with a realization. "You're the fucking Phantom Mel told me about, aren't you? The white-faced man." He looks down at the white mask lying on the table. "I didn't even think to put the two together."

"Because you thought she was crazy?" I retort, already knowing. My own man that I had infiltrated into their kingdom told me her entire family believes she's mental. I don't entirely disagree, considering how she ran into the storm with a fucking death wish. That's three times she's almost killed herself in front of me, and I won't let there be a fourth.

Changing the topic, I don't let Cain answer. He doesn't get to talk about her like he knows her when he was never around to know anything about her. "The Harlots are run by the Whitehart throne. The business side is legitimate, but there's always going to be a few bad seeds."

"*Fuck!*" Duke curses, his head thudding against the wall with thoughts I've already worked through.

Cain rubs his chin, just as pissed as I was when I found out.

Harlots are technically illegal because the three kings couldn't agree that it should be otherwise. The fact that we have one king running the business himself is foolish on his part, but every kingdom has its secrets and corruption. The problem is, we, meaning the Trove and I, don't agree with the law. If women want to use their bodies to work, why should we get a say otherwise? What we want to stop is the corrupted madams who think they can force women into the lifestyle and the bastards who take advantage.

The problem with the throne running the harlots is that we have to be particularly meticulous about how we handle the situation. There won't be the Trove's specialty of infiltrating to kill this time.

"I'll handle it," I say.

"Finally joining up?" Duke asks. They've been trying to recruit me into their Trove for years, since our paths all crossed in the military. While I refuse every time they ask, I help them whenever I can.

I tell them if I survive the rest of the year, I'm all theirs. I've practically been a part of their secret vigilante group anyway, keeping my ears open to any malfeasance that might need correcting and patching up their endless wounds.

Cain hands me what I asked him to bring with a show of rolling his eyes. Duke shakes his head with hatred and disapproval toward both of us.

"If you don't want her to know who you are, what initial are you giving her?" Cain asks.

I shrug my shoulder with the lie. If she wants to damn herself to the *Damned* Prince, at least she can be protected by the reputation.

They're out the door when I hear Cain mutter about meeting with Dragon, their weapons supplier. That's a man I'm thankful I don't work with often. Most would think Cain is the one to fear with his bloodlust, but Dragon is the one who tests his creations personally.

Before the door shuts, Duke turns back. "You haven't seen Dove, have you?"

Dove, the spy of their group. I've only met her a handful of times, while Duke and Cain, the infiltrator and the killer, respectively, are the ones who call on me more often.

I tell him no because she begged me not to tell him she's here, and I like her better than them. Whatever she's working on, she doesn't want the Trove to know, and we're all allowed our secrets.

The look Duke gives me tells me he doesn't believe a word I said. Knowing him, he isn't going anywhere until he finds her.

Chapter Nine

Thump!

I groan.

Thump! Thump!

Grabbing a pillow, I shove it over my head. That's a mistake. It feels like a carriage pulled by the kingdom's largest horses trampled over my temples, turned around, and had another go at me, and just for the hell of it, decided to kick me around until my brain turned into a dizzy mess. Not only is the pain unbearable, but my arms are too sore and heavy to hold the pillow in place.

Thump! Thump! Thump!

My eyes fly open. When the distant pounding doesn't sound again, I attempt to sleep away my agony. I don't know how long I'm out before a low, never-ending whistle grates my ears.

I toss and turn for what feels like hours, pulled from my nightmares filled with bloody hands and daggers by the interrupting thumping, whistles, and I swear I heard a woman shriek.

This time, I jump out of bed with immediate regret when my room sways beneath my feet. On shaky legs, I make it to the door and throw it open, meeting the hard back of my tall, brooding bodyguard.

FATEFUL CHANCE

"Can you please keep it down? I'm trying to die in here."

He raises a brow without muttering a word, remaining unmoved from his statuesque assumed role beside my door.

I shut it and flop back on the bed when it hits me, how in the hell did I get back here? The last thing I remember is my mind in a haze, coming in and out of consciousness with my Phantom's fingers between my legs, his tongue waking me from a nightmare. But if I did imagine that, then the last thing that might have been real was drinking at the tavern with Holden.

I pull the diary from behind the vanity, its newest hiding spot. I didn't write anything in it, but I do have two notes that I haven't seen yet.

Next to a pressed carnation reads:

If the voices are telling you I'm not real, then why do you only tremble under my mouth? Why can't your fingers make you writhe and cry out for God like it's the start of our eulogy?

And the next is written next to a pressed dandelion:

You might not know my face, but behind the mask is a man who sees you. You question if I'm a dream, but close your eyes, and you'll feel me under your hands, in your mouth, on mine… Dreams don't leave the salt you taste. Phantom was the perfect word to call me, little Reaper, because even after my heart stops beating, I'll be on the other side, holding together all those broken pieces you think you are, putting them back together until you're standing by my side, cracked, but wholly mine.

My fingers trace my lips, remembering the feel of him in my mouth, the bitter saltiness that was on my tongue while I was on his. Other than the phantom memories, there's nothing tangible that tells me last night was real, and the fact that I don't remember how I got back scares the hell out of me. This is why I don't drink.

Then again, Dove said she saw him, that she *always* sees him. My palm slams against my forehead. I had him naked with no cloak to hide behind, and I still didn't get a look at his hair or anything that could give me something to look for in every person I cross.

Maison appears at my side, his light brows furrowing as he grabs my arms and thumbs where bruises run up and down my forearms. "You're going to tell me who hurt you."

I study them, growing more alarmed, when I realize they're charcoal handprints. I don't remember anything, imagined or not, that could have caused this. Not even my Phantom grabs me this roughly. "I honestly don't know what could have caused—" My attention shifts to the uncovered mirror behind him, my heart spiking at the crimson-dripping word in the reflection.

Leave

Without a word, Maison rushes toward the washroom and begins removing it immediately, telling me not to worry about it or to mention it to anyone. He tells me it's just candle wax, and whoever left it wants me to panic. "It's probably that cunt, Aspen," he mutters under his breath, his arms working furiously to remove the threat.

"Dinner is in fifteen minutes!" my guard announces from the hallway.

I can't believe I slept all day.

Hurrying to the washroom, I find the Grim Rose dresses on the counter with the carnations on top. I clean myself up, fix my face the best I can without the mirror, and start brushing my hair, but whatever is on it leaves my palm hot and sticky.

FATEFUL CHANCE

"Need a hand?"

I jump back at the sound of Silas' voice behind me. "What are you doing here?" I tighten the robe around me. He takes the brush from my grip, looking at it with the same disgusted grimace I had a second ago.

"Just seeing if you were still alive." His offered smile only reminds me of the harlot I saw him with at the tavern.

"Unfortunately," I pause to take the brush back from him. Before I can say the rest of my quip, he uses my hold on the handle to pull me into him, searching me with a deranged look that holds more black than hazel.

"Don't joke about dying, Eva."

I yank myself from his hold, taking a few steps away to ensure he can't invade my space again. Any time he's near, we end up too close together, and it's muddying my thoughts. "I wasn't. I was going to say, unfortunately, you are too."

"Right." His chest visibly sinks, tossing the brush and a box of brownies on the counter. There's a dour in his features that doesn't belong to him as he turns to leave without his usual witty remarks or mirth.

Good riddance.

I don't wait to devour the heavenly treats in peace. The sugar is exactly what I need to comfort me during this horrendous hangover.

Once I'm perfectly dolled up in the black and jade dress, I grab the carnations and hang them over my door. It's not roses, but hopefully they keep away whatever poltergeists startled me awake, whoever left the threat on the mirror, and any unwanted princes. Witchcraft has never interested me. I like tangible, sure outcomes, like revenge, but I can't knock it before I try it, I suppose. Mel would be proud.

I slip into the dining room as guests are finding their seats. The loud announcement that dinner is ready doesn't help my pounding headache, but at least I don't have to mingle. All I want is to devour whatever animal they've prepared tonight before crawling back into bed.

The nap cleared my head enough to see straight, but my entire body feels shaky with a thick fog clouding my every thought. If I were home, I would have been able to skip dinner altogether, but with King Tydas here and the wedding only a couple of weeks away, I'm required to attend every formal dinner as the central topic of conversation.

Sitting at the round table, listening to the useless chatter of Tydas' daughters telling Aspen about the men in their Kingdom who apparently have a strange infatuation with feet is entertainment I didn't realize I needed. Did I hear that right? Feet?

You like to kiss death, hypocrite.

You mean ride him? I joke back to the voice, remembering one of her past innuendos on the matter.

On my left, Tydas and the king are discussing how infuriating it is to raise girls compared to boys. According to them, girls are too needy and require more money to get rid of, while boys are simple; they hunt, fuck, and have heirs.

There are murmurs between the guards. Digby still hasn't turned up, and another one of them is missing. It takes me a minute to realize it's the happy one who smiles and winks anytime I pass.

FATEFUL CHANCE

The champagne in front of me clinks, pulling away my curiosity. "Hair of the dog. It helps with the hangover," Holden says next to me, a servant already refilling his glass.

I lean in, ignoring the alcohol. "Do you know how I got back here?"

"That's what everyone wants to know." His grin holds a hint of amusement. "Aspen and I searched all over for you, but the kitchen staff said you left out the back. By the time we got here, you were already asleep. No one saw you come in."

My body grows hot thinking about what could have happened that I don't remember.

I lap up the last of my water after taking the final bite of my salmon, potatoes, and broccoli. Nothing is satisfying my hunger, thirst, or the pit bottoming out of my core.

"I'm glad you made it back." He slips something in my palm and offers me an amber wink. "At least celebrate that you didn't die out there."

I clink my glass with his and pretend to drink the bubbling drink, letting it touch enough of my lips to look real. I will be damned if I let someone pressure me into drinking again, even if they offer a handsome smile.

When I open my hand, I find two braided cords of dark silk and leather. "You always wear those cuffs around your wrists, but you don't seem like the kind of girl who favors fancy jewelry, besides that ruby."

I don't get a chance to mutter a simple thanks before Aspen pulls him back to the conversation with Tydas' girls.

Looking down at the bracelets, I'm torn between gratitude and fury. When his hand falls to my knee, a wave of pleasure rolls through me, while I equally want to knock it away. The asshole might be sweet enough to give me gifts but he also read my diary.

Our phantom does that, too, and we still want to sit on his face.

"You have to try this," Silas says with a voice as rich as velvet. He doesn't ask before shoveling potatoes and salmon on my plate with the white sauce I can't get enough of. My heart does a little dance at the extra food. From the look he's giving me, I think I actually squeal.

Trying to be as elegant about it as I can, I devour the plate within seconds, every bite better than the last. My mouth melts.

The smirk sliding up Silas' face as he switches my empty water with his full one says I was anything but elegant about it.

Ass.

Beautiful, helpful ass.

Is it hot in here? I fan myself with my hand as a trickle of sparks work their way up my leg where Holden's fingers softly tap. The air hitting my face feels like angel kisses gracefully placed on my warming cheeks.

Feathers or spiders, Eva? That harsh voice fills me with a deep sense of dread. I push Holden's hand off me with immediate regret when the pleasure disappears, but gentle touches unsettle me. The soft tickles make me want to scream and scratch until I bleed, so new, fresh skin can heal over.

"I have something for you." Silas pulls a small black box from his pocket and drops it on the table, his eyes closing as his fingers trace up and down the velvet material. I reach for it, needing to feel the texture on my skin.

FATEFUL CHANCE

"Oh my! Is that the ring?" One of Tydas' girls shouts from behind me, her voice screeching against my headache.

Every eye is on us.

"I didn't mean to cause a scene." His whispers against my ear steal a breath from me. With a sharp inhale, I take in the vanilla scent against his jaw. His hand on mine sends a jolt of pure ecstasy running through me at the touch, one that has Silas' eyes slant with the same heaviness I have.

Using his free hand, he flips the box open and quickly slides the ring down my finger. The black metal is cold, dragging down my skin for what feels like an eternity of pure bliss. It's intoxicating—hypnotizing. The glistening gold-set ruby is a twin to my necklace.

Every sense I have heightens with a stimulating rush of desire.

"They look like they're about to fuck on this table," one of the girls whispers behind me.

"I'd stay to watch," another one says with hope.

King Tydas rises from his seat. As he speaks, neither Silas nor I look away. Our eyes and hands are glued on one another with a force too strong to tear from. "Prince Silas and Princess Evangeline, I want to wish you the happiest of marriages. My own daughters have already been spoken for, however, I do hope our alliance with King Whitehart here will align our own Kingdoms as well. I have—"

Loud explosions go off with bright lights in all corners of the great hall. My body is thrown back from the blast, pressure falling on top of me, keeping me from breathing properly.

Loud blasts burst again as the entire manor fills with chaos.

Chapter Ten

I can feel arms wrapping around my shoulder, trying to haul me onto my feet, but the ground is shaking too fiercely to stand on my own. With gray smoke burning my eyes, it's too dark to tell which way is up or down.

I cough again and again, trying to clear my lungs. They burn. They burn so bad I fall back to the floor, but someone catches me before I can.

I can't see anything, but I do hear a door slam shut.

The blasts and screams mute behind the barrier. Whatever room I'm in is dark, but there doesn't appear to be any smoke. I can at least blink and breathe without debris making it damn near impossible.

"Eva!" Someone grips and rattles my shoulders. "Eva! Are you okay? Breathe."

A match flares. It's Silas' hazel stare that greets me. They're filled with alarm, searching me up and down.

"Where are we?" I manage to ask through more fits of coughing while Silas lights a few candles and places them on the shelves around us. With the faint glow, I see the room is small, with bottles of wine layered on the floor next to supplies of food, healing salves, and bandages.

"Secret room. It's safe here." He lifts my chin, moving it in different directions. I know it's to check for wounds, but I can't stop the soft moan that leaves my lips at the contact. My body is still too hot and sensitive.

"The others—" I start. Silas stops me with furrowed frustration etched on his perfect face. His hand lowers from my head with traces of blood. I'm suddenly aware I have the prince alone yet again. I could easily kill him and claim he succumbed to a wound he suffered from the bombs.

"They'll be fine. You aren't, though. Stay still," he orders the last word with a finality that had my knees buckle to obey any command of his.

What in the bloody thrones is wrong with me?

"For starters, you're bleeding."

Did I think out loud again?

"Yes, evil princess. You tend to do that when you're tired."

I bite my lip, watching him gather what he needs: bandages, salves, a bowl, and water. He works with a quick efficiency that comes with experience.

His throat bobs with the soft chuckle, inches from me. "You've called me handsome, beautiful, and said something about wanting me to flip you on your back again, only without the blade at your throat." His lip falls for the briefest second.

I wince with a thick, trembling groan when the damp cloth presses against my forehead. "Where did you learn to do this?" I ask, not even bothered that he heard the voice in my head speak obvious lies.

His grin tilts to the side, making me throb in places I shouldn't be. "Promise you won't judge me?"

My curiosity piques. Making fun of someone for knowing the art of healing isn't something I would normally do, even if it is typically a woman's role. "Sure," I agree. He doesn't look convinced.

"My father taught me and my brother to hunt when we were young. Knowing him now, I'm not surprised Holden took to it naturally, but it did surprise me that he escalated the sport into something it shouldn't have been. I felt so awful for the things he did that I asked my maids to teach me everything about healing. No surprise, they didn't take me seriously because I'm a male." He pauses, wringing out the bloody rag, and continues dabbing my forehead. "Then someone almost died in front of me, and I couldn't bear the thought of never being able to help someone like that again, so I made them teach me everything, including stitches, which you won't need this time."

My chest tightens at the possibilities of his meaning, the insinuation of what his brother is capable of, none of them pleasant.

His eyes shift, studying me for any hints of judgement, but I'm lost in his, hyperaware of his fingers still on my forehead. "Thank you." He watches my lips form the words.

My body is heating to an unnatural level. I can feel the sweat on my forehead, can see the sweat on his, the flush in his cheeks. It's a shame a man who looks like him has a reputation for misery and tragedy when everything about him screams the opposite. He bakes for the town and learned to heal while other men live for the brutality of hunting or are hungry for the power that comes with status. He's too tender and caring, and yet he's hard with muscle and carries a dagger on his hip at all times. He's all the things: power, strength, and tenderness.

That spot between my legs throbs in a way I don't think I've ever felt before, not by simply standing still. I shove his hand away, needing to bridge the space between us, but when I grab his wrist, I'm floored with a wave of euphoria that leaves me breathless.

More. Whatever that was, I need more, and it only hits when our skin collides. Rather than ridding myself of him, I grip him tighter, sliding his hand from my forehead, down my neck.

"Why—why does this feel so good?" My eyes roll back as his fingers interlace with mine. I don't even care that I hate this man; I *need* him to touch me.

"Eva..." There's a groan in the back of his throat as he drawls my name. His hips press against me, but he's still not close enough. "I think we were drugged. That comb of yours had something on it."

"I don't care," I say with absolute honesty and pull the strings from the front of my corset. "You wanted me in your bed, right?" He's not my Phantom, but I can't wait for something that might never come, something I can't trust is real. I've never known a need like this. "Fuck the bed."

He abandons me, bracing the wall on either side of my head.

"Is this about the harlot you were with? Is it her you want?" I don't know where the jealousy in my voice comes from, but I don't stop rubbing my arms and body against him, needing any sort of friction on every part of my flesh.

"I don't mix business and pleasure."

"So, you *didn't* sleep with her?" I scoff, but even that comes out ragged and sensual. "I'm sure that's what everyone says when they're spotted with them. What is it they do then? Read to you?" I quip, succeeding at removing my dress. The little black slip I'm left in feels like a thick wool coat.

"Are you jealous, evil princess?" His voice is music to my ears, the soft, low hum dragging me deeper into the burning need wreaking havoc through my core.

Yes! I picture the voice pouting with envy.

No! I'd never be jealous over him.

He chuckles as if he heard my internal tantrum. I don't have the mind to care right now. Not as his fingers brush the choker around my neck. A touch I never would have imagined enjoying as much as I do right now—not from *him*. "You're so warm." His palm falls to the curve in my collarbone, gliding over my shoulders like he's molding me together. "And soft."

I return the favor by tracing the scar around his throat. "If I promise to sleep in your bed tonight, will you tell me about this now?"

He looks me over with hooded eyes. His arms tense as his hand collars just under my neck to crane it back. "That story you have about me in that pretty head of yours is wrong. I'm not the one who gave you the scar beneath this necklace, Eva." His lips brush my temple. "But you're the reason I have mine."

I beg him for more, and with the added pleas, I'm not entirely sure what I'm asking for. I need him to explain everything just as much as I need him to keep touching me.

"Which do you want more, answers or my hands?"

Fuck his choices, passes my mind. That instinctive thought disintegrates because it's the first choice that I don't mind having. The first choice anyone has given me in which I want both more than I want to breathe. I'd happily give up all of the air in my lungs and join the ghosts in this manor if it meant he'd touch me while whispering every answer in my ear.

I don't tell him that, though. I can't wait any longer, can't let him tangle me into a web I won't be able to get myself out of if he keeps talking like that. As if he's giving me control. I *have* all the control.

Lifting my slip to my navel, I lower my fingers to the spot I need touched the most, relishing in the fact that his hold remains against my neck. Holding back the urge to tell him, 'tighter,' takes effort.

It's not normal, Eva, I remind myself. I save those fantasies for my Phantom. The only being, real or not, I can be myself with.

"Give me answers," I pant. The strap slips off my shoulder and he's there. My nipple is wet and cold where he takes it into his mouth, wrapping his arms around my hips to hoist me up.

My legs wrap to straddle his waist, my back pressing against the wall. "Tell me how I'm wrong. Tell me you weren't the one who kidnapped and starved me." His groan vibrates against my skin as he moves to devour my other nipple, his tongue swirling and teeth grazing at the perfect pressure. "I saw you there. You were the only face I saw."

"They kept you tied up and drunk, with a sack over your head for a year. Trust me when I say you didn't see what you think you saw. Not if you're trying to kill me."

I eye him curiously, but nothing indicates he's lying. There is no hitch in the voice, no drifting eyes or subtle twitches. His studying stare holds a desperation, begging me to know some truth he isn't saying while he clutches me tighter, his fingers digging into my ass as he goes back to teasing my breasts with every part of his mouth.

My free hand falls into his hair, fluffing it into the mess of curls I saw in the tavern. There's something about ruining his perfect image that lights a fire in me.

"Silas." My fingers slow to an aching pace between us.

"You believe me, don't you? I can see it in your face." His grin, the way his teeth pinch his bottom lip, brings me right to the edge. "You've known the second you climbed on top of me that first night that it wasn't me who hurt you."

I nod, trying to fight the truth from spilling out. The realization that I tried to ignore. The reason I keep hesitating and finding excuses to avoid killing this bastard. "Because—"

"You're not a killer."

I shake my head. "I wanted to more than anything, but then you opened your eyes, and you didn't look like you wanted to kill me. Like I was someone who had gotten away from you. You looked at me like—"

"Like I'd finally gotten to meet you," he finishes the thought directly from my mind. My legs melt, and it's all him holding me in place between him and the wall. I ride my orgasm with his name riddled with curses on my lips.

"You're right." His teeth tug at my ear. "Fuck it."

He grips the back of my head and pulls my lips to his. To both of our surprise, I open for him while he cups the nape of my neck, bringing me in deeper. His tongue swirls around mine, and that heat in the bottom of my stomach boils, sending my entire body aflame once again.

FATEFUL CHANCE

My eyes are sealed tight when I hear the familiar sound of a door sliding open and closing softly. I can feel the dusky air of the secret tunnels around us. When we emerge in another room, I don't get a chance to take it in before my back hits a soft mattress.

I work fast to rid him of the dark blue tunic while he kicks off his trousers. His skin is so hot against mine, it should be alarming, but as he lines himself up, pressing at my entrance, all concern vanishes.

"You're so wet for me, Eva."

Biting my lip, I can't look away from his tan face and his dark, messy hair. His hazel eyes have me hypnotized until my gaze lands on the faded scar along his neck. I trace it with my thumb. It's much lighter and shallower than mine, but just as long.

He wants to say something; his lips quiver with whatever it is, but I pull him back to my lips before either of us can stop this.

Like in the smoke, I'm not sure which way is up or down, only that he doesn't stop, and neither do I.

"Take me," I say with a heavy breath as pressure starts to fill me. "Please, Silas, I need you *now*." A needy sob tears through me as he does. Pain I wasn't expecting has me gripping his shoulders harder, my nails breaking skin.

"*Fuck*, Eva." He removes my necklace and trails soft kisses along my scar. "I know I said you could be the death of me, but I don't think I can die knowing this feeling exists."

It could be his words, or the fact that he has me more vulnerable than I've ever been; I bring his hand around my neck and tell him to squeeze.

If he kills me, I die, but I need to know that feeling is real, that riding the veils isn't something I'm imagining when I'm alone in my room.

He starts moving again, slower this time. The pain quickly subsides and is replaced with a salacious fullness I've only read about in books.

To my surprise, he doesn't deny me or tell me I'm crazy. His hand slowly applies pressure, testing.

My pants fill with a need for more. I don't know what I need, but I know it's more.

Of *him*.

I don't know what to do except grab his sides as he retreats and pushes back inside me. No book describes the wave of passion that washes over me, the way my vision blurs with the high that makes my head spin, and he hasn't even tightened his hand any further than the possessive hold.

Silas' weight shifts. He pushes back to his knees, caressing my side, looking down at me, at *us* together. His fingers slide up and around my ribs to hold my breasts. I'm so sensitive, when he sweeps over my nipples, I'm brought to the edge quicker than if he were working my clit. "I'd give my life for yours all over again."

His words are a riddle I can't decipher.

Leaning over me, he lifts my leg into the crook of his arm, somehow digging even deeper inside of me.

Being with him is otherworldly. An experience I can only imagine is why spirits remain unrested and continue to haunt this manor. I think if I died here, I'd stay to be near him, too.

"If you want me to choke you, I will." He wraps around my throat again, pressing on the perfect points that leave me struggling to catch any air. My back arches with him sheathing himself inside me, blurring the world with soft, hazy edges. "But, you need to tell me you trust me. That you believe me."

"Sil—" *Thrust*. Every retreat is little reprieve when he sinks deeper into me, carving his own brand where only he can reach. His hold loosens, letting a sip of air reach my lungs.

"I trust you!" I shout. And I mean it. I never would have believed that coming to this dreaded manor would have started with me holding a dagger to his throat to kill him only to find myself begging him to choke me while he slowly pulls the life out of me.

When his hand tightens around my neck, pinning me to the bed as his hips drive into me, the burn in my lungs coils. The other side comes into view. The dark shadows that have haunted me my entire life beg to overcome me.

"Come back to me, Eva." Air rushes to my lungs as beautiful, ethereal light fills my vision, and my core throbs around him. Grabbing the nape of his neck, I pull him to my lips. The noises he's ripping from me coats every kiss between us as his thrusts slow, and his body stiffens.

"When I said you'd stay in my room tonight, this isn't what I had in mind." Holden's tight voice carries through the room from where he's filling the doorframe, covered in dust and blood. "What the fuck do you think you're doing?"

I sink to hide myself under Silas, who is already moving to cover me from his view. Both of us look around and realize we're in Holden's room.

"I think I was fucking *my* fiancé." His brows are tighter than his jaw, with a light smirk that splays across his perfect face. *Checkmate*, it says.

My stomach plummets. "You did that on purpose." I smack his chest.

His attention turns back to me, but the smirk is gone. "I got turned around. Happy coincidence my little brother gets a message."

"I'm not a fucking game!" I roll from under him and grab a pillow to cover myself with. Both Holden's and Silas' eyes fall to the blood that drips down my thigh.

That's when I notice Maison behind Holden, his face tight with a murderous rage I've never seen before.

"*You* might not be, but we did have a deal." Holden crosses his arms and turns toward his brother with a sly smile that's too wide. "I'm sure you can find one of the whores to cuddle you tonight, brother. Evangeline is staying here."

"I drank everything you said!" My voice shakes.

"I said you couldn't drink all three *and* one more beer."

My mouth drops, hanging open without words. He tricked me.

Neither of them stops me from rushing to the washroom.

I'm not going to cry.

It seems like you're going to.

I don't bother telling the voice to shut up as I take a towel to clean myself. Without any clothes, I wrap myself in another towel, bracing my hands on the edge of the counter in front of the mirror.

FATEFUL CHANCE

When the door opens, I'm about to scream for whoever it is to leave until I see Maison. A sight that warms me in an instant. "Don't let them see you cry, princess." He comes up behind me, cups my chin, and lifts. "Do you need me to kill them?"

I almost choke on a laugh that doesn't get past the thickening in my throat. "You always told me I needed to be more careless and live, but I didn't know it would hurt so bad."

Maison's face has never looked so sullen, and I hate that I'm the cause of it. Almost as much as I hate myself for giving myself over to Silas, for letting him have whatever left the gaping hole inside of my chest. For trusting him.

"Maybe it's time you reclaim something else that was taken from you."

Water pools against my lash line, but it has nothing to do with Silas, his brother, or the humiliation slowly withering me into nothing. Maison is right. I can't let every man in my life have every piece of me. My father took my youth, my captor took my sanity, my brother took himself from me, Silas took my trust and virginity.

Lifting my downward gaze to the mirror, my eyes latch onto the scar that stretches from one end of my neck to the other. The dark violet line never faded because of the depth of the cut. The brutality of it.

Looking at myself in the dress shop was different. Growing up with Mel is the only reason I didn't have a panic attack at the quick glance of myself, but even that took years to get used to. I couldn't look at her for the first few months after I was returned, but as the months and years dragged on and her face, *our* face, grew older, it was easier to look at her without wanting to vomit.

CRUEL KINGDOMS

Seeing myself now, my dark tousled hair, my watering eyes, the flushing glow in my fair skin, the hurt visible in every piece of me... I'm not the little girl who was kidnapped ten years ago.

"What do you see?" Maison asks, keeping his hold tight around my shoulders. Next to his sun-kissed skin, yellow hair, and blue eyes, I look sickly. Frail and exhausted, yet held together by a stubborn resilience that refuses to let me die.

During my captivity, I was kept with a bag on my head, except when my captor wanted me to see his 'masterpiece' as he called me.

Sight or sound? He'd ask. Sight meant he'd take the bag off and hold a mirror to my face, forcing me to see the gaunt, weak little girl he made me into. My eyes had sunken, my cheeks were hollow, my lips were cracked, and the color in my face was whiter than snow. Sound also meant scent. He'd eat food next to my ear so I could hear and smell what I was starving for, only giving me one single bite of an apple a week.

If my captor didn't like my answer or I whimpered a little too loud, I was given alcohol instead of water. A burning whisky, a tart champagne, a bitter ale, or a sweet mead. He didn't have a favorite so long as I was out of my mind.

But I'm not in that room anymore.

"Someone I don't know," I answer honestly as something catches the corner of my eye outside the window.

Peering over the windowsill, my stomach lurches at the sight I hoped wasn't true. My father's men are running from the manor into the dreary woods, disappearing into the night. No one would be able to identify them in the plain colors that don't fit our kingdom, but I know. I've seen them set out to do this very thing before.

FATEFUL CHANCE

Every man in my life is making my head ache.

Pulling my hair back into place, I tighten my hold on the towel and hold my chin high.

"A deal's a deal." I toss Holden a pillow where he's pulling the sheets off the bed. "You'll sleep on the floor, fully clothed, and I get all the blankets. That's your one pillow. And I can leave as early as I wish." Turning to Silas, I stone my hatred. "You got what you wanted. You can leave. You weren't invited anyway."

"Eva…" Silas attempts a step forward, stopping when I hold my hand up. My knees buckle from the soreness between my legs, but I catch the bedpost to steady myself.

Silas' fists clench at his side as if to keep himself from doing something he'd regret, like touch me. If he so much as lays a finger on me, I won't hesitate to grab the knife off that desk and ensure there isn't enough skin to patch back together.

"For a second, I thought I was wrong about you, but you proved yourself more cruel than I thought." I swallow hard, forcing that lump to the bellows of my core. "Leave."

Without another word, he turns and follows Maison out with a soft click of the door behind him. I turn back to Holden, who has the bed undone and bare.

"Don't worry about the sheets. I'll sleep without them just fine." My voice is too flat for someone filled with such anger and embarrassment. With hate and confusion. Rejection and betrayal.

"I have a new set here anyway. It'll only take a minute." Holden tucks in a corner of the new sheets. I grab the other end to help move this along faster, needing a nightmare to take me away from this one.

When it's set, I curl and barricade myself under the covers. It almost feels as if I'm not in a strange man's room. Someone I barely know. A man who said he'd help me kill his brother, only now I'm questioning everything about ten years ago.

Silas is right; I had a bag over my head. I've taken the words of my father to fill in the gaps for me. He confirmed that Silas had been the one to kidnap me as some power move to prove his place as heir when the rumors about him being the Damned Prince made his younger brother, Holden, the more desired option.

The confusion running through me makes me shiver. How could I sleep with the man I was sent to kill, the man I was so sure had tortured me? How could I let him use me as a move against his brother?

When Holden emerges from the washroom, his skin and hair are dripping wet. A sight I force myself to look away from. If I were truly evil, as Silas suggests, I'd have half a mind to call him back in here to watch me and his brother on this same bed to prove my own point.

You barely have half a mind and no point to prove. He bested us.

Even the voice in my head is disappointed in me.

"Why did you want me here tonight?" I ask, keeping the blanket over my head.

"Why would I want a pretty princess in my bed for the night? That's a silly question." His voice is farther away than I expected, probably lying out by the fire.

"Did you expect…" I'm not entirely sure how to phrase the question as shame rises to my cheeks.

"I expect nothing. I would tell you not to trust him, but I can see my warnings might not be very effective."

I peek from under the covers, finding him exactly where I figured, lying in front of the fireplace, his ankles crossed, a hand behind his head with the other resting on his naked, toned torso. "I don't trust anyone."

"Didn't seem that way when I walked in."

"I don't have to explain myself to you."

That's right.

"No, but you did see him with the whore, didn't you? He frequents them often." He lets out an exasperated exhale. One I understand the depth of, being the bane of my family's existence. "Like I said, I wouldn't trust him if I were you."

My stomach fills with acid.

"When you're ready to get back at him, you know where to find me." His dark eyes meet mine from across the room with a promise I'm not sure I want between us.

The door opens and Aspen slams it behind her, walking around to the other side of the bed in her red nightgown. "Silas sent me here," she huffs with irritation. I scoot over as she tucks herself beside me. "No, I'm sorry, he *demanded* I come here, or he'd fire all my guards and cut my hair. I would say pleasant dreams, but I hope you both have the most horrid nightmares for making him threaten me."

With Aspen here, I won't be getting any answers I planned to, but that's just as well. I'm not sure I can believe a word he or anyone else says anymore.

Holden snickers, but I find no humor in anything as that gaping hole in my chest is either icing over or shattering all over again.

Both.

Phantom

Seeing blood trickle down my little Reaper's legs turned my vision black.

No one else should have seen her like that. The look of hurt and betrayal on her porcelain face is something I'll never rid myself of.

I didn't miss the bruises on her arms, either. I didn't leave them, so how in the fuck did she get those?

What I do know is she won't be staying in that room.

I slip out the hidden doorway and thank all my luck that she's on the side I need. Holden's back is to me, and Aspen is out cold.

Eva doesn't stir when I lift her into my arms and sneak us back through the secret passage until we're in her room where she belongs.

She's still wrapped in the thin towel when I lay her down on the mattress and tuck the sheets around her.

She's so pale, more so than usual. My fingers find that pulse point on her neck, confirming the steady rhythm that tells me she's alive. That's all that matters.

As I turn to leave, her small hand catches mine. Her soft whimper strains my ear, prickles my skin into high alert.

She doesn't say anything, just pulls me hard enough to send the message that I can't protest. Not when this is all I wanted to do since seeing her bleed.

Noticing the tear slip down her cheek, I wrap my arms tighter around her. Eva doesn't cry.

"I'm fine." I barely hear the lies she's mumbling to herself.

I've sewn skin back together, set bones back in place, and held Duke's insides together with my bare hands, but not being able to help Eva is the one thing that might actually tear me apart.

Kissing her shoulder, I repeat her words back to her even though I know she's not fine at all.

If thinking of me as the Phantom who haunts her pretty little mind is what she needs in order to silently weep to herself, if staying unreal and haunting her in the night helps her through this, makes her feel safe and protected, then I'll stay this way for as long as I have left.

Chapter Eleven

The rest of the week goes by in a blur, mostly because I'm too exhausted to know what day it is. Something has woken up in this manor since the day I returned from the tavern. The whistling and thumping are a constant throughout the night, only now I swear I hear faint whispers and scratches that sound like a cat is scraping through the walls. Every morning I wake to the same *leave* written with crimson wax on the vanity mirror.

It seems the hanging flowers above my door and bed aren't doing anything for the unrested spirits that remain in this damned place, though it's doing a wonderful job at keeping Silas away.

Not ready to face him again, I stay mostly in my chambers while the manor is being repaired, eating hot soup that's sent to me every night, oatmeal every morning, and reading every book that's on the vanity. I swear, just when I think I'm done, new ones appear to ensure I'm never bored.

That was until today, when Aspen dragged me out to visit the town. Since Holden is away on some hunt and two more of her guards have gone missing—the one with the glasses and the one who always looks tired—she begged for the added company.

Her last two remaining guards are paranoid and whisper *witch* behind my back, considering I'm the only change they've had. As if I can take down a beefy guard on my own. I'm at least a foot and a half shorter and a minimum of one hundred pounds lighter than any of them.

I make myself comfortable in the tavern, eating potato wedges and watching Aspen pass out books to random women from afar. At one point, I find her posted near the well on the edge of town, looking like a girl about to wish for her true love to find her. Every woman who approaches her takes a book, pulls out the bookmark to examine it, and then leaves without a word.

It's odd, but who am I to judge?

Aspen's guards are dressed in plain clothing within eyesight and a few steps away in case anything happens to their precious princess. Again, I find it odd, but one can never be too careful. One look at me and no one would suspect I have five daggers strapped to my body.

My own grumpy ass guard is standing outside the tavern door looking every bit like a built beggar which is unconvincing to say the least.

My stomach has been twisting all day, watching the back hall, waiting to see if Silas returns with more women. The anticipation has only led me to order two heaping plates of the salty potatoes. I'm about to order a third when a large presence fills the empty stool beside me at the bar.

"Your father wants a word." The voice of the plain-looking man raises the hair on the back of my neck. He's one of the men I saw running from the manor after the attack, my father's man.

"He wants a word?" I take a breath to keep my anger from flaring in public. "I sent letters demanding a word all week. What's with the secrecy? Why not send a carriage?" I gave all my letters to Maison, who would have ensured my father received them.

"There's tension between the kings after the attack on the manor. Your father didn't want to give King Whitehart a reason to hold you and be perceived as having an upper hand." He clears his throat and quickly gives me a glance over, seemingly okay with what he finds. "You came out alive and unharmed, so quit acting like a damsel in distress. Is there word on who might have caused the attack?"

I shake my head and give him a knowing look. "I heard a guard mention King Byron and King Tydas are sending spies to other royal homes to listen for anything useful."

"Good." He nods. "Keep your eyes wide and ears open. I'll get you tonight outside the gardens. I can't take you far, but he'll meet you in a secure location to talk." Without another word, he drops a coin for my meal and leaves.

"What a gentleman." Maison's mocking voice makes my heart swell. I want to leap to my feet and hug him so tight he'll shatter against me, but I'm too angry at him for disappearing on me all week. Turning my head, I take the childish choice and give him the silent treatment.

My sights land on the grumpy guard outside the tavern. With a thought in mind, I stomp toward the exit, fling the door open, and copy his guarded stance beside him. Crossing my arms gives the effect of a girl throwing a tantrum, but the chill in the air is still making me shiver too hard to do anything else.

"Why don't you like me?" I ask before his bitter face can change my mind. I'm not sure what I expect, but a grunt isn't it. "Hello? Did you hear me? What is your issue with me?"

The guard's stern eyes shift to meet mine, the rest of him remaining forward, like those paintings that always have their eyes on you even as you're walking away.

"He doesn't favor women," Aspen answers, coming from down the alley. "And he doesn't care much for talking either. I like to think he has mommy issues. She probably hit him when he was bad or talked back, and that's why he looks at all women like he wants to murder us with his bare hands."

The playfulness in her harsh words give me pause. This is much more of the girl I first met and not the sweet one she's been trying to portray over the last two weeks.

"Don't bother with him." Aspen threads her arm through mine to leave. "Now, back to what we were discussing earlier, and please don't take this the wrong way, but your wedding dress needs to be a little bigger. We only have two more weeks, but I'm telling you, the tailors are dying to alter what we have to accommodate you."

"I already have a dress in mind." I lie. In truth, I didn't think I would make it this far without killing the prince. And now I only have two weeks left? It's so soon and yet too far away.

Aspen rolls her eyes. "Are you still on about this Grim Rose? She's not even a known designer." The back of her hand caresses my forehead. "Are you sleeping okay? That's the only explanation to cause this ridiculous, *deranged* thinking."

Actually, we hear the ghosts haunting your home, have nightmares of bloody hands, and imagine a phantom holding us to sleep every night before we jerk awake every hour, but please tell us more about how ridiculous and deranged we are.

She means well.

"Her creations are simple and elegant, and yet there are so many little details of lace and—" I stop myself from actually picturing my dream dress.

FATEFUL CHANCE

"Are you at least going to have a veil?" Aspen whines.

I smile, thinking of Mel and how she would be whining about... well, everything. Mel hates thinking about details, especially for parties. She has always been more of a shrug-and-hope-for-the-best kind of girl, while I pour my heart into the smallest of details.

Maybe it's the thought of Mel shrugging, or Aspen's pleas, or the images that spark when we discuss the wedding in any capacity, but I drag Aspen inside as we approach the intimate boutique.

Strix beams behind the counter as we walk through the door, dropping the scissors in his hands and making his way around the counter to embrace me tightly. "How are the dresses?"

"They're wonderful. I was going to wear one today, but Aspen rushed me this morning. I came to ask a favor." I wring my hands, nervous he'll say no. "It's a tad last minute, and I'm not sure if you have anything, and I'm sure you're busy, but I was hoping you might have a wedding dress I could wear?"

"She's rambling," Aspen interjects immediately. Her observations swivel around to take in all the colorful fabric around us. I wince, painfully ashamed of her clear distaste in front of the owner. "It's her wedding. It's royal. I highly doubt you'll have anything—"

"Nonsense." Strix waves his bandaged hand through the air. "Tell me everything and I'll have it ready by next week."

I nearly choke in shock. "Are you sure?"

"Absolutely." He beams, taking my hands into his. "It would be an honor to style you again, Eva."

Aspen pleads with me to change my mind the entire walk back to the manor, claiming the materials in the shop looked too cheap to be suitable for royalty, let alone a royal wedding. She only lets up once I claim to have a headache and need rest, relenting with a yawn that maybe she's right, and my mind is a bit deranged with the lack of sleep and worrying about the missing guards. I add a little wrinkle to my forehead and make a point to tell her I'll see her in the morning so she knows not to bother me for the rest of the night.

After my guard takes my dinner plate and I finish one of the books on my vanity, I make my way through the secret tunnels and sneak into the cold night.

The gardens are excessive with willow trees hanging over benches, old hedges I'm sure are in shapes of animals during the summer, rows upon rows of decomposed bushes, wilted flowerbeds, and barren trees—a garden graveyard during the winter months. Bleak and yet full of rebirth beneath the hardened soil.

I make my way to the stone wall that marks the end of the property. Sure enough, an X is etched into it, exactly where our rat had said. It was to be my escape route after murdering the prince. It still could be, I suppose.

Pushing the stone away with all my strength, I step to the other side where Maison and my father's man are already waiting with horses. I don't get a chance to jump on Maison's. My father's man ushers me to his and helps me on. "We have to hurry." He settles behind me and sets off. "It's not far, but I should warn you he's not happy about anything that has happened."

"I would assume not."

"You need to keep your lips tight and nod in agreement," Maison yells from his horse beside us with thoughts I already have.

FATEFUL CHANCE

The fact that my father's man is warning me sends a spike of fear and trepidation straight through my bones. If his man is brave enough to warn me, things are much worse than I thought.

I figured we would stop in the middle of the woods, but to my surprise, we ride off in the direction of the town. As it grows closer, I think we'll ride straight through, but the horse slows and stops in front of the tavern. I'm about to ask questions, but the look Maison gives me tells me it's wise to stay quiet, starting now. His usual friendly face is weary enough that I bite my lip.

The bustling tavern is a dreary sight at night. It's empty and drenched in darkness as we walk through and to the back room that I saw Silas enter with the harlot. My father stands by the empty fireplace, his hands behind his back. The pretty harlot I saw Silas with is in a robe, sitting at the vanity.

"Evangeline." My father's disappointment is evident in the way he accentuates every syllable in my name. The door clicks shut behind me. "What are you doing?"

He doesn't look at me while he speaks, as if the mere sight of me will disappoint him even more. I know not to answer yet.

"You were supposed to kill the Damned Prince, and yet you're to marry him in a few weeks. I thought maybe you had a plan, but it seems with every passing day you fail in your one task. Tell me, do you *want* to marry the Damned Prince? Is that why you hesitate?"

"I'm not hesitating."

You did.

He turns to face me, predatorily slow. "No? Then why is he not dead?"

"The timing was off. He's surrounded at all times. Even in his room, he's never truly alone."

"And yet…" Every step sends my heart beating faster than before. "I've had reports that you've been alone with him many times."

"No."

The noise comes before the pain. I start to reach for the sting on my cheek but know better, fisting my hands at my side instead. "Did you say no? Are you telling me that my reports are wrong? That I need to *replace* them? Or are you lying?"

"Did you bomb the manor?"

His laugh twists the knife in my back a little more. "I tried to give you another opportunity that you failed at noticing as well."

I attempt to steady myself, taking in a slow, measured breath. "I didn't fail at noticing it. After my first night here, I realized that maybe I should go through with the wedding. That it could solidify our two kingdoms, and with it, their connections would become ours. King Tydas already has a liking for me and has expressed his interest in aligning with us once the wedding is over. If you had read my letters, you would have known."

The second slap fills my mouth with blood. The third doesn't come. Maison catches it before it can strike.

My father's cold black eyes burn into mine, calculating my every movement, every breath, squinting to study me for any hint of lies. That is his specialty, knowing secrets and tracking lies. He taught me everything I know.

"I didn't send you here to think, Evangeline. You have one task. Kill the Damned Prince."

FATEFUL CHANCE

He fists my hair and yanks my neck back. My forced smile comes naturally as I nod my understanding.

The graceful harlot stands from the vanity to grip my father's arm with a feathering caress. "The girl has a point, my king. The kingdom's connections would become yours, but only once she and the Damned Prince marry. Let's say Eva finds herself pregnant with his child. Those connections would be solidified by blood."

My father looks upon the woman who is stroking his arm sweetly. "You want me to whore my daughter out for a connection with the Sea King?"

"Not just the Sea King. The Crooked King and the Scarred Prince have been known to pass through, more so of late."

My father's lips lift. That pull of my hair tightens ever so slightly. "We have a change of plans, Evangeline."

Phantom

Eva's sitting in the forgotten cemetery, thinking she's alone while her mind is spiraling. Her mouth is moving with her internal arguments, but it's too low for me to hear clearly.

I don't need to hear her to know what they are.

Seduce the prince. Marry the prince. Once you're pregnant, kill the Damned Prince.

Her father is giving her four more weeks to complete her task, or he's going to find a way to get it done himself.

His murderous plans don't bother me in the slightest. It's the fact that he ordered Eva to seduce a man he claims kidnapped and tortured her. A man who terrorized her into isolation and made her unable to look at her own reflection. A man she thinks turned her mind into a psychotic mess, where she hears voices and creates a fictional Phantom to make her feel safe.

Snap! My foot breaks a twig.

Her head whips toward me.

"Are you crying?" I ask, coming out of my hiding spot behind the willow tree. I didn't see the glossiness in her eyes before because I was too focused on trying to read her lips.

"I'm insane," she mutters, keeping her back against the headstone with her arms wrapped around her knees.

"That's no reason to cry."

"I'm no better than one of Silas' harlots…" She shakes her head. "I can't have his… You must… But he kidnapped… Did he…"

I fall to my knees in front of her and grab her ruby cheeks, one redder than the other from the slaps her father gave her. If Duke wasn't there to hold me back, I would have blown our cover. The asshole stayed here to search for Dove, just as I predicted he would, and decided to help me with the harlot issue after all. I can't say I blame him; I've been distracted by my little Reaper.

Her lips quiver like they want to keep talking, but she bites them before she can. The cut down the center splits back open, and a drop of blood falls down her chin. "Do you trust me?"

"I don't trust anyone." Her voice is bitter—broken.

She can't see me smile, but I do anyway. "Good." My reply takes her by surprise. "But you need to trust yourself, little Reaper. Don't listen to your father, Silas, Holden, or anyone."

"I just want to know the truth." Her hands fall on top of mine, squeezing in a silent plea as she rises to her knees. "If I can't think straight, how am I supposed to trust myself?"

"I'd argue you think better than the rest of us. Most are too afraid of their intrusive thoughts, but you've made friends with yours."

There's always been a deep honesty within her that I admire, one she doesn't realize she has because she hides behind the voices. But it's all her, the voices, the thoughts, the innuendos—all Eva.

She studies the slits in the mask, trying so hard to make out the person beneath it. With the night sky and no lights near us, there isn't a chance she'll see who I am.

"I wish it was you."

Her words slash through me like the dagger she has hidden in her braid. Her fingers start to lift the bottom of the mask, but I stop her with a quick shake of my head. "I don't think you'll like what you find."

She pushes me back and settles herself into my lap, her legs falling on either side of me. "Then leave it on." Her fingers fumble along my tunic, unbuttoning it one by one. I grab her wrists, but when she looks up at me with quiet desperation and says, "I *need* it to be you."

I'll never be able to resist this woman. I'll carve out my heart and hand it to her if she asks.

I let go. Pulling the knife from her hair, I cut her dress down its center with enough precision not to cut her skin. She gasps with a horrified pout, but I tell her I'll buy her all the Grim Rose dresses she wants so long as she doesn't stop.

I hate that I have this stupid mask on.

When her breasts meet the cold air, all I want is to take her pebbled nipples into my mouth, to tease them with my teeth and tongue until she lets out that sultry groan. I roll them between my fingers instead, as she works to pull me free, stroking me a few times before I take over.

She's slick and ready by the time I'm lining myself up and pulling her down on me, stretching her inch by inch.

Her heat makes me too aware of the sharp chill in the air.

Slumping forward, she claws my shoulders gasping into my neck. "You feel…"

"Unholy," I finish for her.

Her warmth is all I want to be surrounded in, and as much as I want her to ride me, this isn't the position for someone who's mentally and physically exhausted and not that experienced.

Tearing off the leftover fabric still clinging around her shoulders, I take one last look at her, her glowing pallid skin, teardrop breasts that fit perfectly in my palm. I pull her braid free and quickly unravel it.

I'm reminded how truly breathtaking she is when she lets herself be free and smile. The flush in her cheeks might be from the chill in the air, but the pupils that take over the green in her eyes are because of me. The healing bruises along her arms have faded, adding to the obscure lure that is her. In the grim cemetery, she looks like she belongs here.

Pulling out of her is torture for us both. The moment her warmth is gone, I hurry to turn her around, bringing her back to me. "Hold the headstone."

The second she does, I bring her hips to the angle I need and drive back into her, living off every heavy sigh and groan she gives me until I'm sheathed perfectly inside.

"Do I feel fake to you, little Reaper?" I draw back, hovering at the edge of her. "Are you ready to accept that I'm real?" I drive in with enough force to make her tremble beneath me. "That it's *my* cock buried inside of you." Holding her upright, I retreat and press back into her with newfound purpose.

With every growing thrust, she's sliding closer to the cold stone, her front molding against it as every answered whimper sends me into a frenzy I can no longer control. That need to claim her overtakes me as I sink deeper, drive harder.

The questions fuck with her mind. She thinks that come morning, she'll convince herself that she had a salacious dream she touched herself to again, but not tonight. I want to be her Phantom forever, but after her father's meeting, I realize just how dangerous that is. The danger *she's* in.

I trace the empty space on her back where I planned to put my mark. Duke convinced me to wait, not only because he hates forced branding, but he reminded me how resourceful Eva is at keeping herself safe, even when she doesn't realize it. "Tell me you're mine."

Gripping her waist a little tighter, I force myself to take her slow. With the snow melted away, I don't have to worry about her dying of hyperthermia this time, and if this is my last night with her, I want it to last. I want to remember every second with her.

I withdraw and slide back into her, hard and unhurried, gluing my groin against her to get as deep as possible.

"I'm yours." Her legs quiver against me with the ragged sigh she releases. Her foggy breath rises above us. Her arms shake. She's not going to last as long as I want.

Reaching around, I cup her breast. She's so sensitive, I can feel her tighten around me the instant I pinch her nipple, teasing them at the same agonizing speed I'm filling her with.

I love how sensitive she is.

FATEFUL CHANCE

"Are you going to come for me, little Reaper?"

Her pussy's strangling me before I finish the sentence. I was right. Her arms give out, and I have to lie her down on the cold grass to chase mine.

I don't let anyone touch me, let alone during sex, but it's *her* hands roaming my ribs and chest. She'll be the only one who's ever had the chance and will ever get the chance.

I'd let her take any blade to me so long as it's her wielding the weapon.

My instinct is to pull her arms above her head and take her fast, but I don't want to with her. I drive into her at an unhurried speed, dragging this out as long as I can until her eyes are so hooded I think she's going to pass out without me having to hold her pulse points. "Say my name."

"I don't know——" Her throat bobs, and I know she knows exactly who I am, her brows pinching to work through every memory.

"You do." I kiss the tip of the scar on her neck, lifting her leg in the crook of my arm while her hands continue to roam my back.

The moment her eyes meet mine, I toss the mask and pull her lips to mine before she gets a chance to see my face. Her mouth parts, inviting me in. Our lips, our tongues, all of us melt together as I devour her before everything changes.

I spill inside of her, as she clenches around me again, my name filling the ghostly air.

There's no going back.

When she pulls away, her brows draw together, her eyes seal tight, and I don't know if she's horrified, relieved, surprised, or accepting something she's known all this time.

"Silas."

Little Reaper

Silas' face is the epitome of calm, but I see the flash of worry pass over him the second I say his name.

I'm too in shock, too exhausted, to do or say anything else.

Pressing his back against the headstone, Silas wraps his arms around me and pulls me into his lap, gluing me against him with a possessiveness that matches my Phantom.

"How— Why— But, I—" The right question isn't forming as I take in the sight of the white mask lying next to us. The sight that's brought me comfort all these years while I straddle the man I've hated even longer. "This can't be—" My palm slams against my temple. "Wake up."

He grabs my wrist, keeping me from striking myself again.

Silas. The Damned Prince. The man… the man I… "I hate you."

The twitch in his lips turns my stomach into a mess of confusion. "You can tell yourself that all you want, but we both know that's a lie."

"You used me and then…" I mentally strain trying to puzzle together the new pieces. He didn't leave me alone with Holden, and he didn't let me stay the entire night either. The Phantom came back—

he came back for me and held me all night while I cried because of him. "What game are you playing with me?"

"No game, little Reaper. I wanted to come to you all week, but you've been avoiding me and locked your doors. I didn't want you to feel unsafe if I came in through the secret passages as myself." His grip around my wrists loosens, and I realize I haven't even attempted to climb off him. "Just like I knew my face would trigger you after your kidnapping, which is why I wore the mask when I checked on you. I didn't even know you found comfort in it until…" He pauses to grab the mask, holding it between us.

He doesn't have to tell me how he knows. We've been writing journal entries back and forth for years. He's read my innermost thoughts, called me beautiful, given me tips on my dagger-throwing and sparing form, and left me flowers.

I grab his neck and trace my thumb across his scar. "Please," the word catches in my throat, "please tell me what happened. Why were you there that night?"

He doesn't hesitate, and I can't ignore the sorrow that falls over his beautiful face. The hazels that dim, the grin that tightens, the jaw that grows rigid.

"I was kidnapped and tortured ten years ago, too. It was a year until I was able to escape. I walked for days, completely exhausted, until I found a house. It was a brothel. That's where I found you. When I opened the door to the room you were kept in, I thought it was a demented kink, but I heard you crying under the sack on your head, saw the blood around your tied wrists. I pulled it off and cut you free before going for help." His throat bobs as his eyes fall on my necklace. "But when I came back, your neck was pouring blood. One of the guards who was with one of the women came in and said you were dead, but I knew you weren't, or I hoped you weren't. So, I grabbed his knife and started cutting my neck and told him he needed to save you or he would have the prince's death on his hands too."

There isn't a piece in me that doesn't believe him. The scars on his back, the scar on his neck, the way he panicked when he thought I was joking about dying, and when I threatened to drown myself to get away from him.

It's not him who has my hands trembling. I don't understand why my father would lie, why he would want me to hate this man, train me to be cold and calculated, and send me to kill him.

"I don't know who kidnapped you," he continues with a vulnerability in his words. "After we saved you, the entire place was abandoned, and none of the harlots were seen again. The one you saw me with at the tavern, Raven, she helps me gather any information we can find."

My mind is working to keep up, but at the mention of the harlot, my heart skips. "You can't trust that woman. I don't know what she offers you, but you can't trust her. She—"

"Is paid handsomely to be my spy. I told you I don't fuck her, Eva."

"She works for my father."

The angle in his head tells me that's not the case. "There's a lot to talk about, but I need you to know that nothing made me happier than seeing you on top of me with that dagger pressed to my throat. No matter how this ends, I'll never regret any of the time we shared, as myself or as your Phantom." He lets his words fill me, taking in my every reaction. "My days are numbered, whether you kill me or not, but I can't die without knowing... Why did you try to kill yourself that day?"

"I didn't!" I shake my head fiercely and make the confession that crushes me. "I couldn't kill a bee if it stung me." I lower my eyes, ashamed that everything I believed has been a lie. "That day, I only remember seeing your face and knowing my throat had been slit." I let out a heavy breath, relieved to finally stop lying to myself. "I could never kill you."

"Good." His smile twitches again. His thumb catches me off guard as it sweeps across the cut in my lip. "Then why don't you get started on your other task? What was it? Seduce the prince?"

His grip finds the back of my head, pulling me into a deep kiss that says more than any of the confessions either of us laid out. Before I'm too lost, I pull back, asking the last thing I need to know.

"Who kidnapped you?"

This time, he does hesitate. His hand on my waist tightens to keep me in place. "Your father."

Chapter Twelve

The rest of the week, I find myself in Silas' bed, in the bath, on the floor in front of the fireplace, and on the balcony. There isn't a spot in his chambers I don't wrap my legs around him. It's an addiction I can't and don't want to wean myself from. Something Maison gives me crooked smirks and teasing gestures for, while reminding me that his offer to kill him still stands if I find myself at the risk of tears again.

Knowing Silas is my Phantom, blending the two worlds—the one I thought was in my head and the one I slowly stopped hating—is its own mindbender. It's like believing in the afterlife and finding out that it exists, only to learn that I've been dead for years, and it's not so bad, heavenly even.

I don't struggle to sleep when I'm with him. The ghosts and creaking manor are silent whenever and wherever I fall asleep in his arms.

But with the wedding moving closer as every night passes, the dread grows heavier. I can't kill Silas, but I don't know what to do about my father. He's determined to kill him, and without knowing his plans, I can't prepare us for what's to come. Knowing he kidnapped and tortured Silas, that he's the reason for the brutal scars on his back, makes me sick. If he calls for me again, I'm not sure my daggers won't find a new target. And that thought terrifies me.

Aspen has also weaseled me out of as many wedding preparations as she could. The girl is still very much to the point about everything, but that comes in handy when the planners try to convince me of things I don't want, like an excessive amount of red roses or a giant vanilla cake. For starters, roses are horribly basic and my father's obsession. The thought of having them for my wedding is out of the question. And vanilla? Chocolate is obviously the superior flavor. That is the extent of mine and Aspen's commonality.

Now that she's down to one guard, she's more on edge and very much the girl I first met. Her glares have grown more frequent, and I'm positive it's not about our disagreements on the wedding.

Between Silas helping Duke or away doing princely things, and my attempts to ignore Aspen, I throw all of my free time into getting my guard to smile. The man is impossible to crack. He remains a statue at my door as if his sole duty is to guard that door rather than me, though I do spot him and Maison in the distance from time to time. It's disheartening to say the least. He never takes any cake I offer him, doesn't groan or acknowledge me when I ask questions, and doesn't shift when I read romance books loud enough for him to hear. Not even his cheeks pink when I get to the really racy scenes.

Today is different. I can feel it the moment I wake up and see the dusky sky. The promise of rain rolls through the gray morning, and as much as I don't mind staying inside with a cozy fireplace, a book, and a hot chocolate, something feels off.

Holden returned from his weeklong hunt last night, which only put Silas more on edge, bringing back the tension in his shoulders. After seeing the change, I realize how at ease Silas has been all week. Now he's like a lion who knows another predator is nearby. I couldn't pry him off me this morning, and I would be lying if I said I wasn't still exhausted and sore.

"You're cheery," Holden muses, with his hands behind his back. He, too, is different after the hunt. His smile isn't as sly, and he looks refreshed with more energy in every strong feature he holds.

What? No snarky remark?

I prefer my prince a little more damned.

Both my moody guard and Maison appear more alert than usual while keeping their distance in the courtyard.

My target is set against one of the trees, my daggers creating a star where I've been throwing them perfectly. A week without practice hasn't wavered my skills in the slightest.

"Do I?" I muse, tossing the dagger dead center without looking.

"*Mhm.* Practically glowing." I don't miss the hunger that flashes in his eyes. Something I've always noticed but now quickly dismiss and pretend isn't there. "Your plans must be going smoothly, then?"

"Which one is that?" I take the chance to look closer at the tall prince who's standing close enough that I can smell the unmistakable musk of blood, metal, and pine.

"Killing my brother." I swallow hard, peeking around to make sure no one is nearby as he continues, "He's been winning you over while I was away, obviously, but the death of the Damned Prince is inevitable."

"Why?" I whisper low enough that my guards can't hear if our voices carry. "I know why I wanted to kill him, but why do you?"

"Wanted?" His brow rises. "Past tense?"

Fuck. I still don't know his role in this mess, and the last thing I need is for my change of heart to get back to my father. I make my way to the target with him heavy on my heels. "You didn't answer my question."

"We've already told you, tragedy follows him everywhere. He's not a good man. He may have been fooling you this past week, but you know deep down who he really is."

I do, but I think we have different ideas of what that is. "Why not kill him yourself?" I wonder out loud while retrieving my daggers from the tree.

"It's bad luck to kill blood. But I assure you, if you don't intend to do your job, I'll take on the bad luck for the good of the kingdom."

Our dreaded reality is crashing down on me. Silas said he knew his time was coming to an end. Does he know his own brother is willing to kill him if I don't? I think back to how relaxed he's been with Holden gone and how on edge he was when he returned. He must know.

Without waiting for me to respond, Holden turns to leave me mulling over his ominous words.

I'm more than content with my decision to marry Silas, if only to play out this last dream before it all ends horribly. My father is a *very* patient man, but once he has his heart set on something, he doesn't change his mind. If he wants Silas dead, then Silas *will* die.

It's not until I'm back in my chambers that I can breathe again. I need to think, I need to come up with a plan, but before a single thought can come, I spot a box on my vanity with my journal wide open. Butterflies catapult through my chest. We haven't written any notes to each other since the night I stayed in Holden's bed.

Lifting the lid, my world falls apart and my heart sinks to my feet. For a mere second, I think I might have died until I feel it beat again, rising to an unrelenting thunder against my ears.

FATEFUL CHANCE

Nestled perfectly in the center is a bloody heart, my knife with the S etched into the hilt is stabbed through the center with a note written in crimson on the diary pages:

I know what you've done.
Leave or yours is next.

Chapter Thirteen

My eyes are probably swollen and redder than the ruby around my neck as I throw my door open to search for Silas, needing to know this bloody heart isn't his. I'm not one step out before I'm shoved back in.

My grumpy guard looms over me. My stomach drops, realizing I'm alone with this hulking man who looks down on me like he wants to cut my head clean off with his blade. As terrifying as he is, I'm able to get the one word out, "Silas?"

He shoves past me gently, flipping through the diary on the vanity, and starts scribbling.

I hesitantly step closer to where he's hunched over the desk, his back not completely to me like any good guard. Turning the journal around, I see he wrote:

Stay quiet and keep to yourself. This will all be over soon.

"Wh—Where is Silas?"

His dark, stern eyes look up at me, and I could have sworn there's a flash of plea before his face turned back to the hatred mold. He writes again:

He's not who you should be worried about. Trust no one.

I shake my head, not understanding.

My guard sighs, frustrated. He points to the first line again, pushes himself off the desk, and takes his position outside the door, brushing past Silas. Air fills my lungs as I lunge and wrap my arms around his neck. "You're real?"

"Of course." He pulls me back, looking me over with growing concern. It doesn't take long for him to track the bloody mess behind me. "We're leaving tonight, after dinner."

My reply is a long, deep kiss that I can't deny is real. I don't care where we're going as long as it's far away from here, away from the threats, the missing guards, and his brooding brother.

Maybe that's all we need to do, run away and hope no one finds us.

With the manor still in ruins from the explosion, we take dinner in the king's chambers, where the king, Byron Whitehart, himself hasn't left often. The front sitting room is large enough to fit a smaller table for the family, including the king, Silas, me, Holden, and Aspen. Since there are no visitors, we're all more casual and relaxed, except Silas, who sits with his back straight, in a defensive way, I realize.

"Tell us of the hunt." King Byron points to Holden with a bloody steak knife.

"It's a hunt. What's to tell? I killed animals like the boar we're enjoying now." He shrugs his heavy shoulders with disinterest.

"Killing all you did, brother?" Silas asks.

Aspen's lips lift, hiding it well by taking a bite of her bread.

"What is it you did while I was away, *brother?*" Holden counters. I'm suddenly hyperaware of both men on either side of me, holding knives with white knuckles. I grip mine a little tighter. "Visit the tavern while I was away?"

"Enough." Byron glances at me. "The big one likes killing animals, and your fiancé likes fucking whores. Now that it's out in the open, we can quit with the passive aggressiveness."

"The last one he fucked was in my bed." I seal my dropped jaw at the words Holden mutters under his breath.

Silas grabs my thigh, pulling me closer to him with enough force to drag the chair loudly along the floor. "Watch your fucking mouth, or this time I won't waste the healer's time." The rage beneath Silas rises. I've only seen hints of it behind his threatening smiles, but there is no smile on his face right now. It's pure loathing searing through his unbothered brother.

The hold he keeps on me has my stomach coiling with a rising heat that's radiating off him.

There's nothing worse than making a scene, but right now, I don't care about the three others in the room. I take his face into my hands and pull him to me. His lips remain tight as I press mine against his. It takes a second for him to physically soften, but when he does, I know that whenever the time comes, I'm going with him.

A throat clears.

Pulling away from him hurts in every way imaginable, and I don't do it right away. I wait until everyone in the room understands that none of their words matter before reluctantly returning to the conversation that paused for us, but not before placing one last parting kiss on his cheek. His arm remains tight around my waist with the same message.

"What does Aspen like?" I ask, glancing toward where she's watching the scene play out with a deepening scowl.

Byron looks at me quizzically, but I see a flash of something soft pass over him. The subtle twitch at the corner of his mouth. "You remind me a lot of my first wife."

The one he cheated on? Great.

His head shakes as if he heard my thought. "I know what the rumors say about me, but they couldn't be more wrong. I loved her more than the sun chases the moon." He swallows hard. "Contrary to rumors, I never cheated on her. After years of trying to conceive a child, she convinced me to impregnate a harlot, someone we could pay to be discreet and ship away once the child was born, so we could raise it as our own. We didn't know she was already pregnant with him at the time."

He nods toward Silas, who's watching him and living off his every word. They all are. Holden looks as if the boar came back to life and is dancing on the table, and Aspen is looking at her father like she's never seen him before.

The king's demeanor shifts back into the unshaken stone. Just like Silas, he holds so much more than the strong face he presents to the world. They both let hateful whispers cloud their reputations to build them into cold monsters they aren't.

"You asked about Aspen?" Byron changes the subject with ease. "My daughter likes chaos. Thrives in the rivalry of these two blundering fools. What about you, Evangeline? What sort of mayhem do you bring to this table?"

It's a simple question that feels more intimate in light of what he shared.

"She likes knives," Holden answers with a sense of pride in his voice.

"She likes being proficient at something as dangerous as knives because it allows protection and a mastery level skill that's superior to the common use," Silas corrects, sticking the piece of meat in his mouth by the tip of his knife. "And that's not what he meant."

"No, but it certainly provides enough for me to understand her well enough." Byron nods, impressed, but not as impressed as I am at Silas' keen sense of reading people. Or is it only me he reads so well after watching me all these years? "Knives are often used as a weapon for those who want a closer view of the one they maim. One who finds blades their favored choice of a weapon is said to be one of two things, vain and patient or spiteful and impulsive." He angles his head in silent question.

I lift my steak knife and everyone looks at it as I answer, "I like that you see a knife before you, a clear weapon in your face. You don't bother noticing it if we're eating, and yet, if I hold it like this, it's something you look at with keen awareness that it has the potential to end your life." My lips curl wider than I anticipated at the truth of my words. "And yet none of you are staring at Silas's throat."

All eyes dart to see my other hand holding a fork against Silas' windpipe.

The king's eyes widened at the open threat before a smile spread across his face. One that matches both of his sons. "Vain and patient it is. I must admit, our families have never been allies because I'm not a fan of your father's methods of ruling a kingdom, and his *episodes* leave him untrustworthy, but I won't be angry at having a piece of that madness in my own."

Even the king knows we're a little mad.

FATEFUL CHANCE

A strange sense of pride fills me, an acceptance of sorts. Something I'm not sure I've ever felt, certainly never from my father's praises.

After dinner, Silas stays behind to speak to his father, whispering quickly to me that it has to do with the harlot business he briefly told me about, and tells me to wait in his chambers for him. Apparently, his father runs them illegally, but there are issues with aggressive madams and rough male clients.

I pace his room, wringing my hands with too much energy and spiraling thoughts. Why did I have to show off like that?

My heart tickles, replaying every motion, every reaction again in my mind. It was fun. It's why I fell in love with weaponry, specifically knives and daggers, to begin with. Every time I perfected a move, my Phantom left me notes that praised me, and Maison looked at me with pride that made me yearn to learn more.

I think back to the note left on my vanity. They said they knew what I did, but I hadn't done anything yet. They can't mean my plans to kill Silas. Those have been abandoned for too long. Maybe they know I attacked him that first night.

The door opens and my moody guard enters, holding up a piece of paper that reads:

I have to see the king. Stay here, and don't do anything stupid while I'm gone.

I could have sworn a ghost of a smile lifts on his face, but it's too quick to be sure. "I'm starting to grow on you, aren't I? Was it the last book with the love scene? I have a few more that are a lot spicier than that. You can borrow them to read when you're all alone if you want."

He shakes his head at my laugh and walks away. My mood lifts a sliver at the hope of seeing my grumpy guard actually smile one day.

I turn to wait on the bed when the door opens and shuts again. "If you want the book, it's on the desk. It's the purple one."

When he doesn't answer, I look over my shoulder.

Aspen's guard, the last one with the red, irritated eyes, who is always wiping his nose, scowls at me from where he's bracing the doorframe. "You!" His fingers shake at me. "I don't know how, but I know you did it. All we had to do was kill you, but…" His eyes dart around the room. "Who's helping you?"

I rise slowly so as not to startle him. "I don't know what you're talking about."

His throat tenses, his posture shifting forward to rush me.

He doesn't get a chance. Maison steps to my side, a dagger flying in the air…

My eyes flutter open with the sound of my name ringing loudly in my ears. "Eva!"

A chill runs over my flesh. My shivering breath releases clouds as I take in the familiar room. The table that used to be riddled with daggers is now empty, but the candles are still dim and casting more shadows than light.

I'm in the basement. *How in the hell did I get here?*

I turn, searching for the guard, for Maison, but all I see is Holden leaning against the frame of the secret door I clocked on my first day here, singing my name.

My hand flies over my mouth, muffling my terrified gasp. Piles of bodies lie at his feet at the start of the old mining tunnels.

"There you are." Holden gleams in his relaxed stance, his feet crossed at his ankles like he's been waiting patiently for me to wake up. "I might have been wrong about you." He snickers. "I didn't think you had it in you."

"Have what in me?" I ask, climbing to my feet from where I was leaning against the wall. As I do, I spot my blood-coated hands; the flashes of bloody hands that have plagued my nightmares come to life. "How did I get here?"

"Not sure." Holden shrugs. "I found you unconscious on the ground. Perfect time, really. I wanted to talk to you." He lifts his dagger from his waist and admires the gleaming tip. "At first, I was confused how you could fall for someone like my brother. Why you frequented his room at night, but then I got word of your new task. You're trying to get pregnant before you kill him."

My temples start to pound as the truth clicks into place. "Are you the spy? The one that gave all the information to my father?"

"Who do you think has been keeping tabs to make sure you haven't failed completely? I knew you were no lioness. The name they gave you for winning those competitions doesn't fit either. What was it, Vulture?" He snickers again. "No, you're just a scared little doe. Although, after finding your little secret here, I'm conflicted to make my final conclusion on the matter."

My gaze falls to the stack of dead guards behind him. He can't mean to insinuate that this is *my* secret.

Holden pushes his back off the wall and steps closer, but I have no place to go with mine flush against the opposite one. "I spoke with your father, and we came up with a new agreement. One that leaves us all happy."

My heart leaps. Maybe Holden doesn't truly want his brother dead after all.

That thought disintegrates when I find that sly grin, the same one I see my father holding when he captures a new secret that could ruin lives, telling me I couldn't be more wrong. "What is it?"

"Your father wants my brother dead, but he also wants the alliance that you suggested with King Tydas. You obviously don't want to have the Damned Prince's child, so I'll kill Silas, and you'll marry me." His smirk turns more sinister as he watches me come to the realization that he, in fact, isn't changing his mind about murdering his brother. I swear he can hear my heart tumble to the ground and see all the blood ice over my body at his next words. "He wants it solidified by blood. He's instructed me to ensure your task of getting pregnant is still achieved as soon as possible, by any means necessary."

"Why now?" My voice cracks. My heart is beating so fast, I'm surprised I'm able to speak. "You've known about my task to kill him. You've watched me this entire time and never intervened. So, why are you trying to now?"

There's a shift. All amusement is tossed to the side as a predatory gaze takes hold. The relaxed stance he had is now broad and ready for a challenge. I don't run or look away. He's a hunter, and if there's anything hunters like, it's the chase. "I liked watching you struggle to come to terms with killing him. I could see you never had it in you to go through with it."

I turn my head as his knuckle threatens to caress my cheek. "I would hate to report back to your father that you don't seem to be taking this task seriously. Like I said, he's instructed me to use any means necessary." He continues, grazing my collarbone and down my arm. "What's it going to be, little doe?" He motions towards the dead bodies with his chin. "Let's not forget I found your little graveyard here. When my father finds out you've been killing our guards, it'll be an act of war. A little push from me, and we'll return that explosion to *your* home."

He's out of his mind if he thinks I killed those guards. I can't tell if he truly believes it or if this is some mind trick.

My rising chest betrays how erratic my breathing is, but I hold my chin as high as I can. "If you wanted to fuck me, all you had to do was say so."

He squints, stopping his soft caressing to slam his palms on either side of my head. "Really? That easy?"

I nod quickly, my fingers fumbling to unlace the top of my dress. I only have my sister-in-law Audrey's words running through my mind, keeping me steady and focused: *Men are always distracted with a set of tits in their face.* It made me laugh at the time, but I'm starting to think—hope—that it saves my life.

As my breasts spring free, I'm reminded that Holden isn't like most men. His eyes remain on mine without a flicker of distraction. "You disappoint me."

The air leaves my lungs as I'm yanked away, my feet falling over the other. His grip threatens to break my elbow as he drags me toward the tunnel.

"No!" I put all my weight into my hips, pulling myself back to the floor, screaming at the top of my lungs over my shoulder toward the spiraling staircase.

He picks me up with too much ease. His musty palm covers my mouth and nose, cutting off my ability to breathe and any hope of help as he carries me over the foul-smelling bodies that not even his hand can mask. "Normally, I'd enjoy that sound, but the explosion left this room less secure than I prefer."

My stomach bottoms out the deeper into the tunnel we go. The stone turns to dirt and plywood with lit lanterns every twenty feet.

He shifts his hold, letting me take in a little air through my nose.

"I'll give you a choice." The scent of rancid wine, metallic sweat, and musty mold fills my nostrils. "You can choose to scream when I remove my hand from your mouth, but if you do, I'll take you in a way that won't result in pregnancy and will be a lot more painful for you. Or you can shut your mouth and let me do my job."

Knowing I'm no match against him, I give a quick nod. He tosses me over his shoulder, walking faster without having to drag me in front of him.

There's no calling for Maison. There's no calling for Silas. No safety net in a phantom that doesn't exist to watch over me. It's just me and the Huntsman diving deeper into the dark, humid tunnels.

I've never been so aware of how small my body is, how weak I am, until now, pressing against hard muscle that isn't safe at all, but a danger to my life.

All my weapons are gone because I'm an idiot who decided to practice something I'm already proficient in, thinking I was fine enough to go to dinner with Silas next to me and Maison at the door without replacing the daggers all over my body.

Ten more steps, and I'm filled with a familiar scent that makes my eyes water.

As we near a dead end, Holden kicks the wooden door with his boot hard enough that it flies open and slams against the wall.

FATEFUL CHANCE

I'm overtaken with tears to find faded, corner-curled blush wallpaper, and the handheld mirror on top of the matted old mattress lying on the floor. The putrid tarty scent, musky perfume, and tobacco are stronger than ever.

My throat seals tight, working its muscle memory as the voice in my head begs for this not to be true.

I'm back in the prison I survived a decade ago.

All air is forced from my lungs as I'm tossed onto the mattress. Holden pins me down with his knee on my back, making it impossible to lift so much as an inch.

I don't get a real chance to fight before the sack is over my head, and I'm thrust back into the darkness with the scratchy material irritating my face.

"I had hopes for you." Holden's voice is hardly heard over my heartbeat pounding in my ears as my hands are pulled behind my back. My bracelets are torn away, and the scars around my wrists are penetrated with rope.

"I wanted to see how you would try to manipulate me into helping you kill my brother. If you were smart enough to see I was the spy. I was a bit disappointed when I saw you fuck him on my bed. I had to move my hunt earlier before I killed you both too soon." The feeling of my dress lifting up my back only reminds me that if I scream, he can make this more painful than it needs to be.

My thoughts are flashing too fast for me to take in the feel of his palm running over my skin. A tremor runs through my spine.

No, please, please, no....

Memories replay. A distant, husky voice, the dark laugh, the crisp crunch of apples loud against my ear; the tarty smell of them. My dry lips cracking if I so much as breathed too heavily. The moans and screams I mistook for sounds of pain, counting myself lucky for not being a screamer.

I'm carving your initials in my pommel so I can remember it was your heart I carved out, little Evangeline.

The feather...

"You remember how this works?"

I don't say anything because I do remember. My fists clench, my stomach knots, feeling the feather work down my spine with the softest tickle.

One would think a punch to the gut would be more torturous, but I can vouch for the softness of feathers, and a spider's quick, weightless legs crawling and tickling every inch of flesh is a special kind of torture. I never knew where the tickle would land. My body was on constant alert, eventually growing sensitive and irritated.

"Good girl." The bag flies off my head. He turns me over, keeping me tight between his legs, studying me. "You're cute when you're confused."

His breath smells of tobacco and tastes of whisky against my lips. His tongue plunges into my mouth. I force myself not to bite it off without any other defenses.

"My brother might have claimed you in the technical sense." With my corset already untied, he rips the rest of my dress clean off, still keeping his cold, dark eyes on mine. "But I'm the one who made you. I'm the reason you don't drink. The reason you're full of hate. The reason you learned to love blades." He lets out a powerful, wicked laugh as he kisses the valley between my breasts. "*I made you.*"

Movement behind him catches my eye. My heart leaps out of my chest, seeing Maison burst through the door. "Help!"

Holden looks to the door then back to me. Maison saunters next to him without any urgency. His usual happy face falls into a sorrowful frown. "I'm sorry, princess," His chin falls.

"What are you doing?"

"Who the fuck are you talking to?" Holden asks, but I can't focus on him while my best friend betrays me.

"Maison!" My plea catches in my throat. "Why—"

"Silas' old guard Maison?" Holden's brow rises while peeking over his shoulder. "He disappeared years ago." A sinister smile lifts as his thumb brushes against my temple. "You see him, don't you, little doe?" His chest vibrates with amusement. "No one is here. The building's been abandoned for a decade, so no one will hear you either." His laugh deepens. "It's just you and me, all alone, pet."

I blink rapidly. That can't be true. Maison is standing right there. He...

He's gone.

As Holden reaches over the side of the bed and lifts up a half-empty whisky bottle, I know my mistake and what's to come. I spoke without being given permission.

I open my mouth before he says the words, choosing not to have my hair pulled back or spiders unleashed. I can see his pupils take over the amber in his eyes as he pours the burning brown poison down my throat without a fight. I don't have much in me right now.

He can't win.

Maison's not real.

"You don't know the loss I felt losing you. To watch the masterpiece that I built for a year slip between my fingers." He tosses the bottle and kicks my knees apart, kneeling between them, looking down at me like the masterpiece he's calling me. There's a new glimmer in his eye. "It was never your body I wanted, but I was a kid then. And seeing just how fucked up you are, is giving me an urge I can't quite tame right now, little doe." He reaches for the latch on his pants.

I force my sights on the curling wallpaper, refusing to give him any reaction.

"I'm not real to him, but I am to you, princess." Maison leans over the bed with apologies that I mean nothing.

"Finding you in that forest was fucking fate. I was tired of wrecking the maids; they were too easily breakable, but a princess? An Amaros at that? You were the perfect little doe for the taking." His smirk lifts higher at the memory. "You were my special toy. Breaking you down little by little was the highlight of my every day until Silas found you." His jaw tightens, his brows pinching together. "He was too deranged from his own torture to see me in the corner behind you. To see me slit your throat. It was the hardest decision I've ever had to make, but I couldn't let him have you. I couldn't let him come out the hero!"

With a shake of his head, he returns to removing his pants.

I need to hurry.

"I taught you how to escape ropes." Maison urges next to me. "Every type of knot."

Which only means I taught myself.

Great, can we leave then?

"But he wasn't the hero," I say to keep him talking. "No one knew he saved me. My father said it was *him* who kidnapped me."

"I was wearing his cloak. I always do when I'm fucking with his reputation, making the Damned Prince more damning. Your father kidnapped him in retaliation, but the thing is…" Kicking his pants off, he resettles himself between my legs. My head jerks as far away as possible when he grabs my cheek. "No one truly cared. Both of our fathers had their preferred heirs at their side, the Damned Prince was gone, and your father prefers your sister, isn't that right?" He doesn't wait for me to answer. "No wars were waged. They didn't even alarm the false prince and princess. The world didn't notice either of you missing."

"So what now?" I ask, needing one more minute. "You think people won't notice me missing now? The princess who agrees to marry the Damned Prince makes a lot of conversation."

I can feel him pressing against me. "Have you ever heard the game fuck, marry, kill?" He lifts the mirror to my face. "I want you to watch yourself shatter every second I take you."

It's funny how he doesn't see the determination Silas sees in me. The fire he tried so hard to extinguish, heating to shape and form rather than die. Using all my strength, I pull my hands from behind my back, grab the mirror, and slam it as hard as I can against his ear.

He flings back enough for me to gauge his eyes with my fingers, screeching in pain and stumbling away.

A fragment of the mirror is tight in my grasp as I jump to my feet.

Holding the shattered piece out in front of me, I see my mistake. Holden rises to his feet, his shoulders wide enough to fill the doorframe, blocking the tunnels back to the manor, and is too close to the only other door.

I'm cornered.

"What do we do when we're cornered?" Maison asks. Something deep in my mind prickles.

Attack.

My throat dries. The glass in my grip wobbles, blood dripping to the floor. I tighten my hold as Holden takes a step forward.

That prickling feeling grows, making my insides shudder. Flashes of bloody hands come into my vision.

Every fiber in my being is pressing me to be quick about this, to toss the glass at his head, to swipe at his neck or heart. To hit low because I know he doesn't defend low.

But I'm not a killer. I can't— He's someone's son. Someone's brother. I'm not like him. I can't... I can't do it. "Please, don't make me!"

My father's voice rings in my mind: *coward, soft, weak.* Louder and louder, the words repeat until I'm falling to my knees, my hands covering my ears to make them stop, begging them to leave me alone.

Maison steps to me, his hand outstretched. "Let me," he says.

FATEFUL CHANCE

"Just make it stop." When I take it, the prickles vanish, and the world goes black.

Phantom

Meeting with my father about the Harlots didn't go as expected. When Raven, the harlot I work with, told me that Holden and Aspen took over for the previous madam who disappeared last year, handing out books with coded bookmarks that told each woman who to meet, when, and the types of kinks to expect, I figured the throne, meaning my father, was running the entire operation illegally. It turns out King Tydas does, and his recent visit was to threaten to expose my father for hiring so damn many of them if they couldn't come to an agreement on more illegal shit I couldn't care less about——not right now, anyway. That's why I left Duke with him.

Duke ordered me not to tell Cain anything yet because apparently Aspen and Holden threatened his wife Audrey when she was a harlot and the last thing we need is a pissed off Cain. The man has been known to kill and ask questions after.

When I don't find Eva in my room, I almost leave to search hers, until I see the bloody dagger and trail leading to the hidden service tunnels. I know exactly where I'll find her. The same place I found her last week.

But as I take the final step off the stairs into the basement, all I see are the dead guards. No Eva.

I'm tearing my hair out of my scalp when I hear the faint *"Help"* coming from the old mining tunnels. My feet have never felt slower as

FATEFUL CHANCE

I follow the lights and thickening rancid scents to the dead end, hearing shuffling and voices behind the door.

When I open it, my stomach bottoms out. Not only did I not know the old brothel was connected to our manor, but Eva is naked, her hand spilling blood as she holds something sharp toward my brother.

Then, she's falling to her knees and begging him not to make her.

I don't know or care what he was about to make her do, the fucker's *naked* back is to me.

There's nothing to think about. I pull my dagger from my hip. He must feel my presence because he starts to turn back, but he's too slow. He's always been too big and slow.

Kicking the back of his knee, I watch him drop to the floor. His eyes meet mine, and for a passing second, I see who he really is. A man who not only possesses violent tendencies, who needs to hunt to satiate his bloodlust, but is a predator in every sense of the word.

Sharing blood has never made us brothers. I've only ever considered one person a brother, and he's gone.

"She's mi—"

Eva's whimper blocks out Holden's words. Her cry is all the fuel I need to stick the blade into his neck. Two of us have survived a slash across our throats, and I'm not going to take chances that he'll survive this.

Pulling the dagger free, blood spurts from his neck. His eyes widen in disbelief, his hands rushing to cover the wound, but I'm already making another one on the other side.

His curses that I cheat him when sparring ring in my head. There are no rules in real life. I may have taken him unaware, but whatever he was doing to Eva has her in a state I've only ever seen her in four times. All of them after being attacked.

Holden's body doesn't fall before I'm rushing toward her and asking if she's okay.

The moment the question leaves my lips, I watch her eyes glaze over, her head snapping to Holden, who falls to his knees, still clutching at his neck.

Her grip on the weapon tightens. It takes real strength to peel her fingers free of the death grip she has on what I see now is a broken mirror.

"Eva!" I call, tossing the mirror to the side, quickly pulling my tunic off me and over her.

She doesn't hear or see me, which means she isn't going to remember any of this, just like she doesn't remember killing two of Aspen's guards.

But as much as I want her to get out of this catatonic state, I don't want her to come to her senses in this damn house.

I kick Holden's head, ensuring he's dead, before I pick her up and carry her back through the tunnels, up the stairs, and straight out the front door. We stop only to grab a heavy cloak that I drape over her before we're trekking through the pouring rain toward my cabin.

Once she's settled on the bed and the fireplace is lit, I pat her cheek and call her name. It takes a minute, but when her viridian eyes flash to me, I can't hold back my relief and pull her tight against me. "You're okay."

Her eyes grow wild. Her head whips back and forth to her new surroundings. "What do you remember?" I ask. Part of me hopes she doesn't remember a thing. But the other part, the part that wishes Holden didn't die so quickly, needs to know exactly what happened in that room.

"After dinner, I remember waiting for you. Then…" her brows knit together, trying to fill in what her mind won't let her. Her eyes widen again, snapping to mine. "Holden…" She tells me everything, her father's new agreement to have her marry Holden, Holden being the man who kidnapped her and held her hostage for a year, and Maison.

She doesn't remember watching Holden die or me carrying her back here, but I can see the growing questions behind her eyes before she and that voice in her head speak them.

"I'm real," I promise, kissing her wrist so she feels me. "I swear I'm real."

"Who is Maison?" Her throat bobs, eyeing something over my shoulder. I had no idea she's been seeing him all these years. "I'm sick, aren't I? I thought I imagined you, but I've been imagining him this entire time?"

By the drop in her soft features, I can tell my grief is showing, feeling it as fresh as the day I found him. "I never wanted you to remember." I clear my throat. "Maison was my fr—my guard. I had him return you home when you were stable enough, and he was my spy to ensure you were safe. I told him to watch after you from then on. We would meet every week, and he'd tell me how you were doing." I pause to see her reaction, her hand tightening on mine. "We had the same routine for about a year, when one day he didn't show. I snuck into your castle and found him dead on your bedroom floor. You were catatonic. It didn't matter if I shook you or yelled at you, you wouldn't come out of it, but you kept mumbling that it was an accident and that you were sorry.

From what I could gather, he gave you the dagger and tried to show you how to use it, but it must have set you off and—"

"Aspen's guards? Did I—?" Every second of this conversation is breaking me apart. I planned to take this to my grave to avoid the guilt that's visibly consuming her. I can see it in her glossy eyes, her quivering lip.

I nod. "I walked in when one was trying to kill you, but you stabbed him before he could. You were in that same catatonic state when you started to drag him through the servant passages and tossed him into the old mining tunnels next to the first one that disappeared. That's the only way I found you tonight. I figured the last one must have tried and failed. Anzel was able to get one of them, and I got the other two before they could attack you again."

We couldn't outright kill every one of them, not when we didn't know if they were all trying to attack her, and they hardly ever left Aspen's side. They're my father's most trusted men. Killing them one at a time was tricky enough.

At her confusion, I remember she never knew the name of the guard I had infiltrated in Aspen's group of guards, Anzel. The one I ensured watched after her when I couldn't.

"I'm so sorry." Her voice cracks as she wraps her arms around my shoulders and pulls me into her, placing her forehead against mine. "I'm so sorry I killed your friend. That I'm... a murderer and not right. I'm sick and deranged—"

"Stop." My jaw tightens, pulling her away only so she can see how serious I am when I say, "You don't apologize for anything. Do you hear me? If Maison couldn't stop you from killing him, then he wasn't going to protect you. He knew his role, and he failed. That's not on you. Do you understand? That was his entire job, protecting you." Seeing the sorrow filling her, I add, "Maybe you're not imagining him, and didn't know you're a gifted medium. Maybe he has been speaking to you from the other side. There's no way to know. Delusional or not, you're perfect the way you are. The visions, the voices, all of it. There isn't a piece of you that I don't love."

This is the worst possible time, but I can't wait anymore. If tonight proved anything, it's that there isn't anything I wouldn't do for her and nothing that could possibly make me think of her as anything less than mine.

Grabbing her hand, I kiss the back of it and lower to my knee. "What are you doing?" She asked, followed by a quick, "Why are you asking, idiot?" Even with death and glum surrounding us, she never fails to put a smile on my face.

"Marry me, Evangeline Mina Aramos."

"We're already engaged." She laughs, wiping the tear from under her eye.

"Now. Marry me now. I'm a marked man, and if I'm going to die, I'd rather my last days be married to you for as long as possible.

My little Reaper is an actual angel walking up the aisle. Strix, the man who sold Eva her dress, is the only other man I'll let see her in it. Him and the priest.

I broke into the dress shop to find Strix sleeping in the back. The man nearly pissed himself when he woke to me and Eva looming over him. When he realized we weren't there to rob or kill him, he jumped to help Eva ready herself and came along.

I wouldn't let her out of my sight, so we have all of the bad luck on our side with me seeing her in the stunning dress before the actual ceremony.

I've never felt what I do now, watching her walk toward me. The necklace is gone, as are the bracelets, heavy makeup, high braid, hatred, and revenge, replaced with the white lacy dress, purple chrysanthemums, free hair falling to her elbows, and a fucking smile.

The white corset is decorated with ornamented flowers that disappear down the skirt with sheer material, leaving too many parts of her exposed, but it's fitting considering the flowers I've left for her and the parts of herself she exposed to me, and only me, over the years. The entire walk over, she and Strix couldn't stop talking about the perfect boning, romantic cleavage, and see-through sleeves that start at her elbow and loop around her middle fingers.

I'm too lost in this moment, a moment I never thought was possible, as I slide the black band over Eva's finger next to the round ruby I had made for her weeks ago while I repeat our vows: "I am you, and you are I, we are one, from now to death, through the afterlife, and into the next."

Her eyes light up as she slides the ring on my finger and repeats the same vow.

Before the priest can announce anything, I pick her up in my arms and kiss her. "You're enchanting."

I've always told myself that even if she succeeded in killing me, I'd find a way to be with her. I would come back as a wraith to haunt her until her bones are ash alongside mine, and nothing has changed. I'd watch her, creak the boards of any home she finds herself in to see her flush, whisper to her throughout the night to see the chill slither up her spine, watch the goosebumps prickle along her arm as my ghostly breath graces her flesh. The vows I swore aren't a lie. I will haunt her long after I'm gone from this world.

She's mine in this life and the next.

I carry her bridal style all the way back to the cabin, kicking the door open.

"No invite?" Aspen leans back on the bed with Raven unconscious on the floor next to her. A guard I recognize as King Aramos' man stands guard by the fireplace. "Sit or the whore dies."

—Chapter Fourteen—

Silas' hold on me is more secure than ever with his hands under my thighs, gripping me against him as if we'll die if he lets go.

With the murderous glare Aspen is giving us, we just might. My father's man doesn't move a muscle, his hands clasped in front of him with a self-assured grin, waiting for whatever order my father sent him here with. He's always been the silent one I knew would cause problems one day. Splint, a name given to him for leaving people in them too often.

"If this is your idea of a wedding gift, I think we'll pass." Silas ignores her order to sit.

The princess snaps her fingers. The door slams shut, cutting off the pattering rain and rolling thunder. Before we know what's happening, Splint is tearing me from Silas' hold as another man we didn't see discards Silas' daggers. Blaise, the man who set off the explosions and retrieved me for my father.

Silas twists, his fists tight, readying to take him down with his hands if he needs to. He stills the moment I feel the cold blade against my neck.

"The lady said *sit*," Splint orders.

FATEFUL CHANCE

Silas doesn't hesitate, grunting in pain when the guard strikes his temple with the pommel of his knife, quickly securing his hands behind his back. The blood that falls down his cheek turns my vision black, my father's voice growing louder and louder: *I didn't seed a damn coward, Evangeline! Cold and calculated, that's what we are. You're nothing like your sister.*

Aspen stands from the bed, kneeling next to the fallen Harlot. "You do know Raven, right?" Her head tilts to where the guard lowers me onto the chair across from Silas, all while keeping the blade secure against my throat. It's then that I notice the corked vial on the table between us. "She fucks your husband, but she works for me."

As she straightens to her feet, her face looks older, more poised in an instant. Her black hair that cuts under her jaw doesn't look so childish, but mature. "Tell her."

Raven's eyes shoot open. She crawls to her feet and steps against the wall, looking more timid and shy than she had with my father last week. It doesn't fit her pretty face like the strong, confident one does. "Yes, he makes me tell him what he believes are secrets while he fucks me."

My blood boils. Not because I know she's lying, but because she crossed him. Silas' foot kicks mine, under the table, the point of his boot running up my shin. I don't need to look at him to know he's begging for me not to trust her.

I don't.

Aspen wants to get a rise out of us.

"I knew she was a cunt." Maison appears next to Aspen, glaring her down with disgust and hatred blending with his charming features. "I can kill her for you, like the guards. Let me take over, and I'll have her dead on the floor before you blink and wake up someplace safe."

"No." I shake my head, earning everyone's attention.

Aspen's smile widens with pure joy. "You know, I saw my brother's madness in him at a young age. Call it a gift, but the moment I saw you, I knew the rumors were true. I could see it in the way you look at nothing as if something's there, and the way you mumble to yourself throughout the day." She waves the guard off my neck as she takes the third seat and picks up the vial. "I used to help Holden make these concoctions. We'd mix all sorts of things in your water and alcohol and watch you hallucinate for hours, but this one was always my favorite." The green liquid tilts in the glass jar. "Datura. This time I mixed it with nightshade, aconite, and opium."

"Sleeping death," I mutter.

"At least let me kill the asshole who had the knife at your neck?" Maison pleads desperately.

Oh, yes, please! my inner voice jumps with anticipation.

This time, I hold my tongue.

"I figured you'd want this when we're done killing my brother." My heart falls to the floor at the sight of the knife angled under Silas' hardened jaw. "Your father is insistent on wanting him dead. Claims he's a demon who escaped his hold and needs to be put down once and for all. My father used to tell me about King Aramos' episodes, but seeing it in person is..." She searches for the right word.

"Terrifying," I finish for her.

Her brows pinch with disappointment. "Raven, why don't you entertain King Aramos' men for me?" She nods Splint away, who quickly abandons his stance at my back to drag the harlot to the washroom. The other pouts and Aspen nods him off, too.

"You think I'm a fool, but you're not going to hurt me, Eva. Your father told Holden all about you when he propositioned him in his plan to kill Silas. They actually have wagers—" Her face twists with a gut-searing rage I feel from her stare alone. "*Had* wagers. Your father bet against you killing him, but Holden doubled down. This was all a sick game between wicked men. But I had my own bet with Holden."

Her laugh sounds like an old hag's while eyeing Silas with disappointment. "I bet you'd make a fool of yourself, and the entire wedding would be called off before it happened, but nothing I did worked. I tied your laces too tight, but you ran off before passing out. I sent you to Holden's bath, but Silas didn't even care. I drugged your comb, but that explosive went off before you could make a fool of yourself at dinner. Not even the whistling, scratches, and screaming throughout the night or the threatening notes could get you to run away. Do you know how messy it was to put that pig heart in your room? I put it in my room first to frame you, but my father knows me too well, or believed you too good for such a thing. "

Aspen leans back in the chair, eyeing the poison in her hands. "Unlike what those guards think, Silas isn't going to die." Her dark, cold glare lands on me again, a smile lifting higher up her round cheeks. "You're going to drink this sleeping death, and then I'll let him go."

"No!" Silas' shoulders shift with his struggle.

The chair cracks as Aspen leaps to her feet, gripping his chin tight in her palm with her own knife at his throat, pinching hard enough to draw blood. "Now, Eva." All I can look at is the red dripping down Silas' neck.

"Don't." Silas continues fighting the ropes and now Aspen's hold on him, worsening the cut she's giving him.

I don't hesitate to grab the vial and take it back. It's fitting. He saved my life in more ways than one, the least I can do is save his.

"Come on, Eva! Let me!" Maison screams from the corner.

The moment Aspen drops the knife, I stand. "I can do it myself."

The washroom door bursts open. Raven walks out, her naked body covered in crimson blood as if it were a new dress. "Men are too easy." Her head cocks to Aspen as she holds a cigarette to her lips and lights it with a quick swipe of a match.

I don't know or care what happened in that room; all my focus is on Aspen, who springs out of the door into the pouring rain.

Thunder grumbles through the air as I lift the skirt of my dress and follow Aspen through the trees. I'm not a runner, but I keep up, hearing her calling back. "Why did you have to come here?"

Her black hair flops ahead, maybe twenty feet away.

My feet slip from under me, my knees landing in thick mud. Kicking off my shoes, I jump to stand, but when I do, the world around me sways. The poison is running through me quickly, but I'm not dying without taking her with me.

"I spent too much time getting us where we needed to be for you to come along and ruin it! Do you know how long it took until my father finally got the hint and stopped hiring women?!"

Aspen stops when we enter a clearing. The dark sky replaces the barren trees, and I realize we're at the edge of a cliff. Aspen spins to face me.

"Why?" I shout. "Why do any of this? It can't just be for some wager with Holden and my father!" I pull the daggers from my corset, one in each hand.

"It's about them!" she screams. "They're mine! They always have been! My own mother was the first whore who thought she could take their affection from me. An actual harlot. The plague was the perfect timing to get rid of her, and when I did, I thought that would be it. I'd have my father and brothers to myself. But then those fucking maids wouldn't leave them alone! I had to twist Holden's violent tendencies to see that just fucking them was boring. Then you came along! Holden's '*special project!*' All these years, he couldn't forget you, and then you came back! Even my father has a soft spot for you!"

I can see her so clearly now. A version of myself if I didn't have the Phantom and Maison praising me at every corner. I strived to be seen by my father, but when I had them, I didn't need it as much.

My head spins faster, the cliff's edge teetering just ahead of me. I don't have much time.

"What now? Are you going to kill me, Eva?" Her arms flop in the air with a dark hackling laugh in the black of night.

Yes.

As I grip the knives tightly in my hand, a gust of wind knocks me off my feet as a bolt of lightning flashes brightly between us. I fall to my back, hearing Aspen's frightful scream and a deep *crack* loud enough to pierce my ears.

My vision might be turning black from the poison working its way through my veins, but I see the moment Aspen disappears. I crawl on my hands and knees to the edge and see her body among the rubble, too broken and bloody to be alive.

I can't make sense of anything as I'm lifted in the air and placed on something soft. A fire might be crackling in the distance, but I can't open my eyes to see. Something cold runs down my throat, and I hear Maison telling me that I did good as Silas begs me to wake up.

I can feel the sleeping death taking me deeper to the other side. I only pray that I don't find rest so I can stay with him a little longer.

Chapter Fifteen

My life flashes before me. I'm a child, running around our gardens with Mel before settling under a tree with a book about fairy tales. Then I'm older, dancing with Cain, dreaming of my own ball and wedding, hoping I'll get to choose my own prince, one I truly love and not who my father chooses for an alliance. Those are the rare blissful moments between my father's tyranny: his palm kissing my cheeks more than his lips, the tongue retainer so I know when to hold it, the dancing in burning heels so I know not to follow my brother's footsteps.

I see the moment I'm taken by Holden, the bag over my head, the starvation, the thirst, the cracked lips, the day I met and became friends with the voices that live inside my mind. I remember the day my wrists were cut free and I saw Silas before my vision turned black, and I woke in my bed at home, unable to fully speak for a year.

Then I'm brought to the moment I met Maison. His light hair, cyan eyes, and trusting smile. He came every day and ensured I ate food and drank water, cleaned the bandage around my neck, and spoke to me as if nothing was wrong with me. I shied away from him, but he came back day after day until the tiniest sliver of me trusted that he wasn't going to kill me.

I don't remember the next memory that flashes before me, but I'm stuck in it anyway. Maison hands me a dagger and shows me how to hold it. Later, I'm lying in bed, cradling it to my chest. Nightmares flash of being stuck in that stinking room with the bag over my head, when a soft touch wakes me. I don't think before I stab the blade toward whoever it is, only when I open my eyes, I see Maison. He's telling me it's okay as blood runs down his chest. "I promise I'll be okay, Princess. It was an accident." I can't move. I can't speak. I can't think. I don't know how long I sit there after he's gone. I see my Phantom come in and shake me before bathing me and putting me to sleep, all while I'm unmoving on my own.

I see all the times I trained, thinking Maison was there with me, except I was alone, talking to myself. I see moments where I'm with Maison when others were around and realize that no one else talked to him. The day my father hit me in the tavern, *I* stopped his third slap, not Maison.

"I know you're awake, little Reaper."

My lips lift, not wanting to open my eyes in case this is a dream. Another hallucination.

The kiss on my lips feels real enough that I open them. Silas is at my side, in a bed and room I don't know. None of that matters when I notice the bandage around his neck.

"Just a scratch."

"He's healed your brother and their friends enough times, I figured it's time we repay the favor." Audrey, my sister-in-law, stands from the chair beside him. "Mel wanted to be here, but she left with Cain and Duke last night." Her eyes roll as she cradles the smallest bump around her belly. "Your husband is about as unbarring as mine. Wouldn't even leave your side to shower."

His hands are covered in crimson where they tangle with mine. "I said *if* you did die, there has to be a way to preserve your body until we find a cure to fix you. We could put you in a glass coffin to visit."

"You're so morbid." I wince, trying to sit up. "How long... *Where* are we?" I ask both questions at once.

"Your brothers," Silas explains. "Or the Trove's. It's a place we're all welcome. We don't know who else is under your father's command, so we're laying low for a little while. Raven wanted to stay after saving you, but Mel took one look at her and dragged her off with them."

He has me recall everything about last night in detail, filling in what I miss. When he carried me back to the cabin, Raven cut away my dress, finding the Kissing Cure that's embedded in every Grim Rose dress. It was the start of three days of constant cures that Mel knew how to brew. It turns out Raven didn't betray Silas at all. Embedding herself where she needs to is her real expertise.

"Oh please," My nieces burst through the door, Delany and Alison. The auburn-haired girl, Alison looks at Silas with literal heart eyes and speaks with a voice filled with wonder. "Like you didn't count every hour, minute, and second she's been unconscious. But I will thank you again for bringing Duke back with you. Mel can go to hell for taking him away." She pouts, sounding just like her father, my brother, Cain.

Really, I don't know why everyone despises Mel.

Delany snickers to herself. Her eyes widen when my grumpy guard pushes through the door with his arms crossed in front of his chest. His guard attire is gone, but I'd know that stern face anywhere.

"I didn't know you had a name," I snark, remembering Silas telling me it was Anzel.

"You didn't ask."

"You wouldn't have told me," I say confidently.

He nods in agreement.

"I also didn't know you talked. What was with the notes?"

"People have ears everywhere."

"He wouldn't leave your door," Delany says, looking at him as if she were the twin who loved romance instead of making disgusting faces at them.

Anzel smirks. "It's my job."

***To watch the* door?**

"Always the damn door." I smile at the sight of the little one he's giving us. "I knew I'd grow on you."

Anzel follows to where I spot a book tucked in his hands. Shaking his head, he turns to leave. "I'll give it to you when I'm done," he mutters quickly. The girls and Audrey follow him out the door.

"What's going to happen now? My father's a tyrant. Our Kingdoms are going to——"

"You'll be fine." Maison's voice has me whipping my attention to the door. "You're safe."

Silas turns my head to his, following where I'm staring, where I know there's nothing.

He bends down and kisses me, softly at first, but turns savagely in seconds, like he isn't sure if this is real.

His eyes meet mine with a look I often see him have, only now there are words for it——*hunger, desire, want, need, obsession.*

For the past ten years, I woke up with hate in my heart, training with revenge in my blood, and went to bed knowing another day was closer to killing the man I married. The man I thought I made up and the only man who helped me accept every part of myself, delusions, voices, and evil reputations.

"You owe me a dance, little Reaper."

Epilogue: Silas

One Year Later

Eva's legs wrap around my waist, her rain-soaked slip clings between us as we sway side to side in the dance she owes me for not cutting off my finger during finger roulette. Her feet won't be touching the ground, but I need her to know that she can still enjoy anything she wants, even if it's in a different way.

I watch her eyes drift over my shoulders, where she gives a somber smile to someone who isn't there and mumbles her internal thoughts out loud while I listen with complete devotion.

I wasn't lying when I said Maison deserved his fate for not protecting her. I'll go down the same way if I fail, but I would be lying if I said it didn't kill me finding him dead. I truly hope I'm right when I say she might be seeing his ghost. He was more of a brother to me than my own, and I wouldn't put it past him to take his oaths to guard her with his life to heart.

I don't regret killing my own brother in the slightest, in fact, I'd kill him slower for everything he's done to Eva. I'd tie him up with a sack over his head and pour spiders all over his body, use poisons to fuck with his brain, starve him… I'm happy she didn't get the chance to kill him. She doesn't need any more death on her beautiful, delicate hands.

FATEFUL CHANCE

The very hands that are running up my neck while I waltz us around the kitchen, flour in our hair, egg yolk on her arms, chocolate on her tongue as the rain patters against the window. The bundle of flowers she picked outside of our new cabin is tossed on the kitchen counter next to the unfinished pancake batter.

I couldn't help myself. The moment I saw Eva through the kitchen window, laughing at the sudden rainstorm, I dropped the batter mid-stir and ran after her. She yelped as I picked her up by the back of her thighs, her arms wrapping tight around my neck as if I'd let her fall. I was ready to push her against the nearest tree and fuck her like I did last week, but there was something about the familiar position that reminded me of dancing. About being in that tub when she told me why she doesn't.

We started in the rain, her soft giggles as the tune we swayed to. By the time we got to the kitchen, she thought it was funny to reach for the flour, sending the puff of white into the air around us, and I retaliated with the eggs. After tipping my finger in the melted chocolate and spinning her away before she could reach anything else, she finished the fight by sucking the sweet chocolate clean off me.

I'm only glad no one else is here to witness or hear what I'm about to do to her.

Eva didn't want to live with servants, maids, or guards, though Anzel is the one exception and now lives in our basement. Strix and Raven visit too often for my preference, bringing a mountain of dresses and Eva's niece Delany, who coincidentally has taken up Eva's and Anzel's obsession with romance books. The fact that Eva has one person in her family she's growing close to is the only reason I don't shoo them away.

There's a new glimmer behind her viridian eyes that I'll ensure never dims again.

Listening to Eva recount Aspen's death was enlightening to how dissociated she can become. Eva claims she was aware of everything that happened, that there was a strange chance of lightning striking and killing my sister, but I was there. I watched Eva toss her dagger with perfect precision into Aspen's eyes before running after her and sticking the blades into her heart over and over. It didn't stop until Aspen stumbled back over the cliff's edge. There wasn't even a storm cloud in sight, no lightning, no thunder…

Her pretty little brain won't let her remember the violent acts she's done, and I won't tell her either. While she tried to mold herself into a cold and calculated woman, she's always been a soft, warm-hearted girl, and not in a bad way. I just hope she doesn't start seeing all of the people she's killed like she does Maison.

The other murder I won't tell her about is her father's. It hasn't happened yet, but that's only a matter of time. The fucker burned her, hit her, didn't start a damn war for her safe return, and God knows what else. As much as I love who she is, I want to kill the man for making her full of hate, especially toward me.

Hearing Eva speak about her past is different from her perspective, too. Watching her from afar was just to ensure she was safe, that she wasn't haunted by that year forever, that she lived, learned to throw cake batter, found that thing she loved more than sewing, wore jewelry, and found her prince. And while I prided myself in knowing everything about her, she didn't write everything in that diary, and I'm glad for it because I get to know and see a side of her I hadn't before.

One thing is absolutely certain, I love this evil princess and will rip out anyone's heart that dares to shatter hers.

Tightening my hold, I twirl her around, watching her wet hair whip through the air and the smile spread across her face as her head tilts back before I perch her on the corner edge and drag her legs to opposite counters. Those deep, green eyes fill with life as she reaches between us and pulls me free, her palm stroking me base to tip. I grab a knife from the block and cut away her slip.

Her mouth opens to argue but turns to a sultry moan as I take her budded nipple between my lips.

It's always been a slow seduction between us. A dance between a phantom and a reaper where one can't exist without the other.

"Real," I answer the question hiding behind her eyes as I push into her. Even if I weren't, I'd make the same promise because there isn't a veil thick enough to keep me from her.

Epilogue: Silas

Ten Years Ago

Holden's form is absolute shit.

He's only a few weeks younger than I am, but towers me by three inches with an inch more muscle on every limb, and I'm not a small guy. None of that matters if he doesn't learn to defend low or know where his weak spots are. His neck and ankles, for starters, right next to his massive ego.

Taking my time, I fake low, bringing the wooden sword with me as I pull the other dagger from behind my back, take a step away from him, and jab the wooden weapon straight across his neck.

"You cheated!" he shouts, his cheeks strawberry red with a darkness behind his amber eyes that I only see when it's been too long since he's hunted, or when he sees one of the maids sauntering toward his room.

He either wants to fuck me or kill me, and I seriously hope it's the latter.

"You're too slow, big man." I taunt him, knowing how much he loathes his bulky form for reasons like this.

FATEFUL CHANCE

"Whatever." Holden grabs my sword and tosses it to the side. "I have better things to do besides fuck around with you."

"Oh yeah?" I call after him. "Like what? Fuck a maid? Come on, let's go again. We both know this is the highlight of your day."

He turns, his grin lifting into one I don't recognize. "Not anymore. I caught a special doe that needs my utmost devotion."

My stomach sours, twists, and begs to revolt at the thought of what he does. I've witnessed too many gruesome scenes and never once has he considered his hunts anything '*special*,' more like a necessity to keep his ass calm and leveled.

"Go on then." I wave him off. "I'll take the maids for myself."

The fact that he doesn't retort gives me pause. Holden is territorial to a fault. To the point that I can't have a real relationship with Aspen, our sister, because he's claimed her as his. To be honest, I'm not mad. They share the same mother and blame me for her death, the Damned Prince, who spread the plague that killed her, though, I don't remember being sick when it happened.

I'm about to turn back to the castle when shuffling in the trees sets my ears on alert. Normally, we'd spar in the courtyard, but Holden insisted on the nearby woods for a different playing field.

When I turn around, two men approach, both in basic leathers that aren't traceable to any kingdom and are definitely not our men, but I know the look of someone wanting to spar. Their swords are drawn, leaving me with the wooden dagger in my hand.

I'm ready.

My lungs ache from too many days of grunting and screaming. My back can't decide if it's numb or wants to scream with me as the pain sears through my bones.

I lost the fight days, maybe weeks ago. It was over too fast when three more men came from the woods to play.

"Where is the princess?" It's the one question they repeat before and after every lashing. My abs tighten, knowing it's about to start up again.

I lick the salty sweat from my lips. I've already told them I don't know where Princess Evangeline is, but nothing I say changes their minds. I keep my mouth shut this time.

At first, I thought this was an eye for an eye situation, but my father isn't in the business of ransoms or taking children, even with a rival kingdom that holds many of our secrets. What's to gain? It's beneath him and an act of desperation. *Tacky*, as he would call it.

All air is sucked out of me as the whip strikes my back. I've never given Hell a thought, but I'm confident this is it. The word *pain* isn't a word to me anymore. It's all-consuming. Every punch to the gut, broken rib, cane cracking across my jaw, and leather lashing that slices my flesh is something I'll never get used to. Each one is worse than the last. The only thing keeping me sane is the metallic taste of my own blood. If I can taste blood, then I'm still alive. Right?

The worst part is my hair. It falls over my face, tickling my nose, irritating my eyes…

FATEFUL CHANCE

"Again, where is she?" Every word is drawn out, or maybe my head is too slow. I haven't eaten or drunk anything other than the sweat and blood that drips down my face.

"Who?" I laugh out of pure delirium. My head is too light. The air is too thick and hard to take in. My back burns like I've been flayed open.

"You know who, Prince," the man sneers in the darkness. "Princess Evangeline. Where did you take her?"

I only know Evangeline by name as a girl from a distant kingdom, the sister to whom my father wants me to marry, Amelvira. He wants me with the one who's closer to their father, so I can be close enough to spy for him. Now, I want nothing to do with this twisted family, whether it would make my father proud of me or not.

Their dungeon is as dark and hellish as the family's reputation. I swear, even surrounded by pitch-black darkness with my hands tied behind my back, and forced to sit in the most uncomfortable chair, I can hear the whispers through the wall. All the secrets King Aramos has collected throughout his lifetime. I can smell the rot seeping through every crevice.

I cry out as another lashing strikes my back, this time higher on my shoulder as they taunt me with their endless questions.

This has to be it. Whatever curse has befallen me since birth is finally catching up to me. All fifteen years of tragedy is mine to take on, to rid the world of the Damned Prince once and for all. My only thought is of the princess I don't know, Evangeline, the name that will haunt me long after I pass. I need to know what happened to her and why I'm here.

Maybe I died and this is hell.

Holden must have struck me too hard in the head, and here I am, imagining being kidnapped and tortured for months on end.

That fucking name, *Evangeline*, is going to be the death of me if I haven't died already. I don't even know the girl and she's my own personal reaper—a black cloud looming over me, taunting me further into whatever hazy madness is slowly eating at me.

I've never been one for violence, but part of me wants to find her and take all the breath from her just to give it back and take it again. Like what these men are doing to me because of her. I want to be the only thing she thinks about because she's the only thing I can think of, and I don't even know what she looks like.

Evangeline, Evangeline, Evangeline. That name is on replay. I picture her running away, being kidnapped and held for ransom, eaten by a lion, falling off a cliff... There are too many possibilities of what could have happened to her.

I hope she ran away, so when I get out of here, I can find and taunt her until we're both raving mad.

The door opens. Thank the fucking thrones. It's been too long since they last came, and I'm positive I can't go one more day without food or water.

"You're going to be quiet, or we'll *both* get into trouble. Do you understand?" A girl's hushed voice grates on my ears. "I'm Amelvira, but you can call me Mel. My father is..." She pauses. The softness of her cold hands on my wrists makes me hiss. "He gets this way sometimes. Let's just say he won't remember you're here and his guards don't give a shit about Eva. They just like torturing you."

My arms howl as the heavy shackles drop to the floor with a loud *thud*. I grit my teeth as she tries her best to lift me from the chair. I'm stumbling onto my knees, my face catching the hard stone. All the strength in me is gone, wilted away from months of abandonment.

The girl urges me to hurry as she helps me up, saying something about karma and helping me will bring her sister back somehow. I don't tell her that I don't hold the same faith that her sister is alive if she hasn't been returned yet. It only means my time is limited as well.

None of that matters right now. My eyes ache, sealing together at the bright assault from the candelabra Mel's carrying while taking my weight on her shoulders. It's a struggle, every step is a struggle, and somehow, she manages to drag us through the hallways until she's tossing me onto a bed, ordering me to rest.

I couldn't do anything else if I tried. My legs are practically useless, and there's no fighting the deep sleep that takes hold of me or the nightmare of a pretty ghost promising to end me.

The room I wake in isn't my own. There's too much black and red with soft accents of purple.

It takes all my strength to walk to the door, only to find it locked. There's a plate of food and three glasses of water left on the vanity that I don't hesitate to scarf down, reading the note left for me:

Food will be brought every morning. I'll release you once Eva's returned.
Be grateful it's not the dungeon.

CRUEL KINGDOMS

There isn't one ounce of me that is upset about the new situation. Like the note said, I truly am grateful to not be in that dungeon anymore. The healers who worked on my back were lazy and were only there to ensure I didn't die too soon.

Peering out the window, it looks to be summer. The grass is bright, the trees are full, the sun is high. It looks the same as when I was first taken, which means it must have been a year.

It doesn't take long for me to scope every inch of the room, finding a mix of books on the shelves: princes falling in love with princesses and fathers beheading their daughters for witchcraft. The wardrobe holds hanging dresses, all dark in color, and pastel slips. There's untouched makeup layered on the vanity, as if she keeps getting them for gifts but never uses them. Then there's the painting of a cabin on full display, while the ones of flowers and scribbled poetry are set to the side.

The juxtaposition of this girl is fascinating.

I smile to myself. Sure enough, diaries are hidden under the mattress, hidden in a way only a girl would believe them safe. Taking them into my lap, I settle on the mattress and read about a girl dreaming of finding a prince and love, of hating her father but loving her brother and sister more than anything. The girl wants to break free of her well-mannered and well-behaved, *cowardly* self. She wants to bake and throw the batter around like she once read in a book. She wants to master something useful instead of learning to sew, and wants to be gifted pretty jewelry and flowers at the same time.

Evangeline, you're more interesting than I thought. Typical, but in a way that's not at all boring. My little Reaper is starting to grow on me with every single page of her innermost thoughts. The ones she believed no one else would ever know.

I spot her jewelry box with an idea.

The secret tunnels took me a few days to figure out. The door was too jammed from not being used, and my arms were too weak. I had to slowly work at it every day until it finally budged this morning.

I finish writing my own diary entry for Eva.

Find your prince.

It's the only thing I can think of with my head still hazy and the fever that's making my body sweat more than a sparring session.

Despite what Mel promised, the food wasn't always there when I woke up, and when it was, there was too little of it to satiate me or energize me for more than a few hours, but that doesn't matter. Today's the day I leave this place.

I tuck the ruby necklace I pieced together from the different materials I found around the room and return the diary back under the bed, hoping she makes her way home to find it, and vowing with every fiber of my being that if I make it out of here alive, I'll spend the rest of my life figuring out what happened to the girl who's plagued my every second over the last year.

Sneaking out of the castle was easy enough. The old servant tunnels led me outside, and with the Aramos castle set so far away from town, they don't bother with much security. I only had to wait for the guard to take a piss to make my run through the woods.

The hike back home is brutal. A clouded mess of trees and rivers, birds taunting me, whispering that I'm not going to make it. The sun beating down on me is worse than the whips and fists, melting my skin into the grass that I continuously find myself falling and waking up on.

CRUEL KINGDOMS

I don't have long, but I know I'm close. It's been days, maybe a week, since I made my escape. There's been no sight of another being, no guards following me, no hunters mistaking me for prey, although that's what I am—*weak*.

I nearly burst into tears when I see a house in the distance, hidden between the thick summer trees.

My throat is too dry to shout, but I use every strength I have to stumble toward it, not bothering to knock before I twist the handle and fall to my knees inside. A rush of tobacco, stale wine, and sweat fills my senses.

This is not a typical home, and if anyone were to ask me a year ago, I might have considered this place heaven, but the naked women aren't doing anything for me. They don't glance in my direction, too busy dragging men in and out of rooms, rubbing each other on the velvet chaises, or drinking straight from decanters.

I need water. If I find the kitchen, I'll be able to wet my throat enough to ask for help.

Lifting to my feet, I brace the wall and make my way down the nearest hallway. Doors open and close as moaning and screams fill the shadows. I'm too focused on the door in the back to peek inside any of them. It's like a string has attached itself around me and is pulling me straight to it, only when I try to open it, it's locked.

My heart shatters as I wiggle and tug on it harder.

I need to get in there. Whatever is behind this door is calling to me. I can hear a voice in the back of my mind demanding that I don't live to see another day until I open it.

FATEFUL CHANCE

Taking the nearest candelabra I find, I bash it against the doorknob, panting with sweat pouring down my temples until it breaks.

Kicking the door open, I don't find the kitchen. There is no water or food on the other side, only a stained mattress on the floor, a vanity covered in rotten apples and booze, and someone sitting with a sack over their head in the corner.

I turn to leave. Whatever depraved sex act this is, I want no part of it.

The whimpers stop me. My head whips back to really take in the girl. Her small, slender frame is in a sweat-soaked chemise that leaves nothing to the imagination. Her legs are glowing red with irritation, and her shoulders shake the slightest bit.

Another whimper and a sniffle have me barreling toward her and ripping the sack off her head.

She looks like Mel, the girl who saved me from the dungeon, except with black ratted hair, gaunt cheeks, viridian eyes that are too big for her pale face, and she reeks of alcohol.

My heart doesn't just shatter, it fucking sings at the sight of the girl that's haunted me for a year.

"Eva?" My throat burns as I whisper her name, half of it because I can't get the rest out.

I don't know how or why she's here. I only know she's not staying another second. I'll rip these ropes off with my bare hands, my teeth, if I have to.

I look around for anything that can help, finding the knife stabbed through one of the apples.

I apologize profusely, peeling the crimson rope out of her flesh and working the dull blade through it.

I want to tell her she'll be okay, but I'm not sure she will be. I've never seen someone so small and fragile. Her arms are just bones covered with irritated, pink flesh.

Once she's free and I know she won't topple over, I run down the hall, filled with more energy than I've had in a year, spotting a guard removing his cloak to follow a harlot into a room, and use the last of my remaining strength to scream for help.

He spots me with furrowed brows, "Prince?"

I motion for him to follow me, relieved when I hear his heavy footsteps gaining speed.

The moment I re-enter the room, my entire world sinks into itself. Eva grips her neck where blood is spilling from as she falls to the floor. The guard pushes past me, knocking me to my knees. It's the perfect position while I internally beg and pray to every deity I can think of to spare her. I didn't make it out of that hell to find her only so she can die.

As blood pools beneath her, the guard turns to me, shaking his head.

No.

This wasn't for nothing. She doesn't get to fucking die. We—

The blade on the guard's hip glimmers. I dart for it. My hands shake but I've never been more steady, never been more sure of anything as I hold it to my neck. "Save her."

FATEFUL CHANCE

We're tied together whether either of us wants to be or not. Both of us were kidnapped, starved, and tortured. I don't get to live through this if she doesn't.

"Prince," the guard pleads for me to understand.

His eyes widen as I draw blood across my neck. "Every second she lies there, I'm cutting deeper, with *your* knife. If you don't want to die with us, you should find a way to save her. *Now*."

Eva's been with our healers for weeks now, but today's the day she's returning home. She still hasn't woken up, but they say she'll live.

"Are you sure you want me to go with her?" Maison asks as we make our way to the healer's quarters. He's three years older than I am, a new guard, but we've grown up together since we were children. While Holden had Aspen and they had my father, I had Maison. He's not only my best friend, but more of a brother and father than either of mine.

"That family doesn't give a shit about her." My fury bursts thinking about the lonely, hopeful dreamer I read about in those diaries. "I need someone on the inside to make sure she's okay."

His brow rises as he studies the scar along my neck. "Don't give me that look." I shove his shoulder.

"It's not like you to care about someone else's well-being."

He's not entirely wrong. With the reputation I have, I tend to see the worst in people, the sneers they give me, the whispers they think I don't hear, and the distance they all keep.

CRUEL KINGDOMS

My skin prickles as we enter the healing quarters. The sight of Eva's sickly form sleeping on the twin bed, her neck thickly bandaged, enrages me like no other. She really thought she could take the easy way out of this, but she has no idea what she's awoken in me.

I would watch after her myself, but I'm not sure I don't hate her.

"No one else has mattered." It's the most honest thing I've said. Even if I do hate her, she gave me something I've never had before. A purpose.

A purpose to live in those dungeons so I could find her, and now a purpose to ensure the girl I read about doesn't die in any sense of the word. She *will* find her prince. She'll have that stupid fucking cabin where she'll have those ridiculous romantic gestures, the dancing in the rain, the food fights, pretty poetic words, and all the flowers she can dream of.

His heavy hand lands on my back. "For you, I'll protect her with my life."

ACKNOWLEDGMENTS

I am truly grateful to everyone who has helped bring this book to life. This novella came to me on a whim and spiraled into the idea of an entire series that I could not get out of my head, starting with Sinister Desire. And here we are.

Shayla Marie! As I write this, I am in Virginia and voice messaging you, if you can remember that. I am so glad that you filled out my ARC reader inquiry on Instagram for Sinister Desire. Not only has your feedback been incredibly helpful, but I love Joe-king with you.

Bristin! Words can't describe how much I adore you! Your excitement about absolutely everything gives me life!

That also goes for Kim, Riley, AJ Bryce, and Valeria. I have so many more Beta and ARC readers that I can thank, but you all have been around since I started, so I thank you with my whole heart!

Geena—it's your turn. You didn't even read this until it was published, so you get this little shout-out because I will always love you and will forever be grateful for you listening to my rambling! I tried so hard to hold myself back, but I slipped and you let me talk your ear off while you were at work for hours… so thank you!

Nadia, you got the drunk ramblings of this book, and if you ever read it, I would be shocked, but thanks for all your support.

Nick, thanks for letting me ignore you while I write.

9 798999 245352 2